BLIND SIDED

Danny M. Gray

ISBN: 979-8-89663-125-5

Dedication

I dedicate this to my parents for your constant love and support. I know you are still guiding me.

Acknowledgment

I want to express my heartfelt gratitude to my community, Maple Hill, NC, where I witnessed the transformation of impossible dreams into reality. It is here that I learned invaluable lessons that have shaped my life. The strength of our community has always been evident, as has the love that unites us. It is a place where stories have been shared across generations.

This dream would not have been possible without your unwavering support and guidance. Whether in a church, a field, or simply walking down the road, the voices of my community have always been with me. I am deeply grateful, truly honored, and profoundly blessed to have grown up in Maple Hill. The principles instilled in me continue to resonate, regardless of where life takes me, the jobs I hold, or the people I meet.

Thank you, Maple Hill, for all you have given me.

About the Author

Danny M. Gray is a storyteller at heart, bringing his rich imagination into both the written word and the screen. Born and raised in Maple Hill, North Carolina, Danny draws inspiration from his roots and the people who shaped his journey. Spending time back home has deepened his appreciation for family and the values that continue to influence his work.

As a seasoned author, Danny has penned a number of books, each an exploration of emotions and human experiences. His works span genres, from psychological thrillers that keep readers on edge to heartwarming family dramas that resonate deeply. Through his storytelling, Danny creates immersive worlds that captivate and inspire.

Danny's creative journey extends beyond writing. As a veteran actor, he has brought characters to life in Hollywood productions like *The Hunger Games: Mockingjay Part 1 and 2* and popular TV series *The Game.* His military background lends authenticity and depth to his performances, blending real-life experience with dramatic expression.

In addition to his creative pursuits, Danny has built a successful career as a program manager and consultant. Being a certified Project Management Professional (PMP), he brings discipline and precision to his corporate roles, effortlessly balancing his artistic passion with professional excellence.

Today, Danny resides in suburban Atlanta, where he continues pursuing his dual acting and writing passions. His work serves as a reminder that with dedication and resilience, nothing is impossible. Whether through novels, on-screen performances, or corporate endeavors, Danny Gray invites others to explore the boundless possibilities of creativity.

Preface

The world thrives on appearances. Polished smiles, structured routines, and picture-perfect lives create a fascia that few dare to look beyond. But beyond the exterior lies something far more complicated—a labyrinth of hidden desires, dangerous choices, and carefully guarded secrets. Each decision, each action, pulls at the fragile bonds of trust, threatening to loosen everything.

Steven Blackman has mastered the art of control. To the outside world, he is the epitome of success, a determined professional whose life seems privileged. But cracks in the foundation of his seemingly perfect life are beginning to show. The betrayal of those closest to him sets Steven on a path where loyalty and morality blur, forcing him to question everything he once believed.

Lisa, charming and enigmatic, carries secrets of her own. Her relationship with Peter is complicated, but her connection with Drake, Steven's sharp-witted and ambitious rival, ignites a firestorm of emotions and consequences. What begins as an affair becomes something far more dangerous, roping these lives in ways none could have foreseen.

This is a story of intersecting lives, where ambition collides with vengeance, and trust is both a weapon and a weakness. As truths unfold and motives are revealed, each character is drawn into a web of deception they cannot escape.

In this intricate dance of loyalty and betrayal, there are no easy answers, no clear lines between hero and villain. The choices they make will shape their fates, and as the story unfolds, one question will remain: *Who will emerge unscathed, and who will fall victim to the tangled threads they've spun?*

Step into the broken web, where nothing is as it seems, and no one is truly innocent.

Prologue

"Dispatch, urgent assistance needed! We have an adult male with trauma to the skull and no pulse. We are securing the scene!" Officer Martin spoke into the radio with his gun returning to its holster.

"Can you identify the body?" crackled the dispatcher's inquiry.

"From the scattered mail on the counter, it appears to be a Mr. Livingston. We have not found any other identification," Officer Martin informed, examining a bundle of letters handed to him by Officer Nixon.

"Officer, the ambulance is en route. I have also notified the detectives on duty. Arrival is imminent," the dispatcher's voice conveyed.

"Thank you, 10-4," he responded.

Standing over the unfathomable scene, where Mr. Livingston's body was lying sprawled on the cold marble floor, Officer Martin surveyed for signs of intrusion. There was no visible threat, yet he sensed the unknown haunting.

"Officer Martin, I am going to search the bedroom and see if there is any identification. Be careful with what you touch," Nixon cautioned as he moved upstairs.

"Roger that!" Officer Martin affirmed, opting to explore the living room and the depths of the basement.

After carefully examining the residence, the officers cryptically found an absence of intrusion. As they ventured into the garage, they discovered the car's engine, unnervingly cool to the touch. With the preliminary searches concluded, the officers waited for the imminent arrival of both ambulance and detectives, which didn't take long.

Detective Sandra Becker could be seen getting out of the car with her senior officer, Detective Henry Smith. They made their way into the house, carefully taking in every minor detail that could become handy to confirm if it was actually a murder.

"Detective Smith, do we have any leads yet?" asked Officer Martin, looking at the senior officer, indulged in carefully inspecting the scene of the crime.

"Lisa Blackman is the primary suspect!"

It was not Detective Smith who spoke, but Detective Becker.

***

Contents

Chapter 1: Deception

The Lexus rumbled ominously, its approach echoing through the quiet neighborhood and adding suspense to the European-style home. The slanted roofs, with their subtly flared eaves, were beautifully adorned with a combination of stucco and stone. A soft breeze whizzed through the well-tended lawn outside a moderate-sized house.

With a gradual deceleration, the Lexus slid into the driveway, aligning perfectly with the parked BMW. This familiar scene was nothing new for both the driver and the onlookers in the area. It was a common sight, given the elites residing in the neighborhood.

In mere moments, a graceful figure clad in a black, drop-shoulder dress emerged from the sleek Lexus, strolling up the driveway toward the imposing front door. Ascending the steps to the inviting patio, she cast a quick glance back to ensure her car was securely locked. Next, she pressed the doorbell, a subtle chime echoing in expectancy. Patiently, she awaited the door to swing open, granting her entry.

She looked around, absorbing the opulent trees and shrubs adorning the street. Her eyes wandered upward, captivated by the expansive sky and the tranquil panorama the house afforded. The precisely crafted landscape never failed to enchant her, evoking a smile that held a touch of wistfulness.

Glancing back at the entrance again, she pressed the doorbell once more, impatience bubbling within. Her eyes met a distorted reflection in the frosted glass. As usual, she looked drop-dead gorgeous. Her tight clothes snugly fit her curvaceous figure, accentuating her body in all the right places. The black dress, an outstanding distinction against her dark complexion, heightened the allure. She was aware that her physicality was the only reason men found her attractive, although she didn't mind that. She was comfortable with the men surrounding her underestimating her capabilities because it helped her get her way.

After a short while, she could hear heavy footsteps and the unmistakable thumps of a man's shoes crossing the foyer. The massive doors creaked open, revealing a tall, muscular man with salt and pepper hair beaming at her.

"Lisa, what brings you here? You usually turn down my offers. It's-it's a pleasant surprise," he said.

Lisa's greeting was abrupt. "Hi, Drake. I am not staying. I just brought your stuff back. We need to end this for good. We have to stop seeing each other."

She didn't dance around the issue; it was not her style. Lisa's directness had always left her past partners bewildered, underestimating the intelligence behind her straightforward approach. They didn't think she would have the brains to conduct herself that way.

He didn't expect this reaction from her. He became momentarily silent as he was not prepared for this. Despite his nonchalant conduct, focused solely on his career and friends, Lisa's decisiveness caught him by surprise.

"First thing, those were gifts for you, meant to be yours," he stated with a touch of offense.

He was perplexed by the notion of her returning them. It wasn't as if he cared whether she would keep them or throw them away; he harbored no desire to reclaim them. He simply yearned for an explanation for this sudden shift, as everything was going smoothly according to his plan. He was unable to wrap his head around how she could exude an unexpected detachment.

His inquiry turned suddenly sharp, a businesslike edge cutting through the emotional tension. "Is this your idea or Steven's?"

A solemn calmness enveloped Lisa's response. "Steven does not know about us yet. So, you can say this is my choice. I am still married and in a suspicious loom. I have to focus on my marriage if we are going to make it work. For the sake of saving my marriage, we must part ways."

Her voice held a monotony that belied the gravity of their conversation; to an outsider, it would seem like mundane chatter rather than something serious and profound. However, Lisa's response elicited a delirious laugh from Drake.

"Oh, right. As if he is faithful or like he's some saint. What nonsense is he filling your head with?" he scoffed, suppressing a smirk.

"What? Steven has always been faithful," Lisa retorted, although her conviction seemed to waver.

"You don't actually buy that, do you?" he asked, wearing a mischievous grin. "Why do you think he's still in Mexico? You're clueless, aren't you? It's because of Sophia," he asserted, seizing control of the conversation.

Refusing to relinquish dominance, he deftly manipulated her, determined not to lose her without a fight. He always knew how to manipulate her to get his way.

"Sophia?" Lisa questioned, struggling to maintain composure. The notion that her husband was unfaithful, despite her own indiscretions, was a bitter pill. She didn't equate her actions to his; in her mind, his infidelity questioned her very essence—her beauty, her personality, her self-worth—a narrative she refused to buy for herself.

Drake smirked. "Yes, Sophia Rodriguez. Upper management needed someone to ensure the merger went smoothly," he said, reveling in the control he now possessed.

Lisa hesitated, locking eyes with Drake. Rage surged within her, resisting the thought of her husband entangled with another woman. Drake's explanation seemed plausible, yet doubt crept into her heart. Was he fabricating it to maintain whatever clandestine affair they shared?

"That doesn't prove anything. There's no way, not Steven. He—" she began to say.

Seizing the moment, Drake interrupted, capitalizing on the situation.

"Please step inside. We can talk. I promise to tell you everything," he said, pretending to lower his guard and hoping to earn her trust.

Lisa pondered for a moment. She steeled herself for the worst, resolute not to let her composure slip away.

"Alright, but let's keep it to talking only," she insisted.

"Of course," Drake replied with a warm smile.

Drake was known to be a skilled manipulator. He adeptly crafted an atmosphere that lulled the girls into a false sense of security. Lisa cautiously entered, and Drake, with a gesture of surrender, assured her.

Closing the front door behind her, Drake guided Lisa to his living room as she scurried her gaze around.

"Your place is amazing. I must say I am impressed," she remarked. "The decorator did all the designing, but the outside is a different story. It is one of my hobbies," Drake said, an impish smile playing on his lips.

Lisa halted, realizing she had misjudged Drake. Despite her usual astuteness, she found herself proven wrong by the man she thought she had figured out. She even considered herself somewhat of a manipulator. The minor error in judgment bothered her, unsettling the confidence she usually exuded.

"I like a man with taste," Lisa said in a sultry voice.

Drake reveled in the game, smiling internally.

"There are a lot of things you don't know about me. We only ever got to know each other on a sexual basis," he admitted with a hint of rue in his voice. "Besides, I like to keep my personal life private."

Lisa snorted derisively. "Well, you have done a great job up to this point," she replied.

They resumed walking, side-by-side, through a hallway that extended into a modest living room. The space boasted an indoor fireplace, plush sofas, a massive chandelier, and an open kitchen.

Drake guided her to a plush sofa, gesturing for her to sit. As she sank into the soft cushions, her thoughts shifted to the impending conversation.

"I will get you a drink," Drake offered. Lisa started to interject, emphasizing the platonic nature of their meeting, but he dismissed her objection. "You will need it. I am sorry to have to tell you this, but you will."

He strolled towards the open kitchen, revealing an array of exquisite bottles stored in a cabinet that dazzled Lisa's eyes. Pouring a lavish amount of Dom Pérignon Rosé champagne, he gracefully placed the glass in front of her.

"I am sorry to have bothered you, but with Steven sneaking around as he has been, it is imperative that we put an end to this," Lisa emphasized, underscoring the purpose of their meeting.

Yet, her reminder concealed an underlying motive—she needed to reinforce the necessity of terminating the affair.

"In many ways, I love my husband, and in others, I hate him, but I won't tolerate his infidelity! Now, tell me about this Sophia and how you discovered their affair," she continued.

"Since the last few months with Steven was in Mexico, Jada Technologies initiated a partnership with C-Soft IT Consultants. Sophia is a significant figure in the organization. She's the one who proposed that Steven spearhead the merger. The higher-ups readily embraced the idea for obvious reasons," Drake revealed deliberately, selecting his words to provoke Lisa's emotions.

He aimed to kindle her fury at the thought of her husband's betrayal, leaving her feeling both wounded and humiliated. What an evil player he was!

"The employees there could feel the energy between the two of them—the undertones. I don't even know how to say it, to be honest. But I believe Steven's allure stayed in her mind, thoughts of his near-perfect skin tone and wild speculations about his failed marriage. It was evident that her yearning surpassed mere business partnership." Drake's innocent comment concealed his designed understanding, yet he pressed on.

"Come on, Drake! You are reading too much into it. Just because she admires Steven does not mean they are involved," Lisa countered, attempting to dismiss Drake's insinuations.

"Sophia is really gorgeous. And I bet Steven had fallen for sure; that's why he extended his stay. I knew he'd be occupied for a while, and these things never stay hushed for too long. Now that the merger is at the point of completion, the technical team is there. I know it's just a matter of time before he will be back," Drake explained, confident in his observations.

Lisa sat beside Drake, rendered speechless by this unfolding drama.

"I—" Lisa began.

But before Lisa could voice her thoughts, Drake, fully aware of the tension, closed the gap with a sudden kiss, plunging them into a passionate entanglement. Lisa, initially caught off guard, succumbed to the intensity of the moment. Seizing the opportunity, Drake lifted her in his arms and carried her towards the bedroom.

"Drake!" Lisa stammered, attempting to resist the whirlwind of emotions.

"Shh!" he hushed, and Lisa surrendered to the magnetic force, losing herself in that moment.

Drake was easy to love; he had a gift for effortlessly charming his way into love, weaving an enchantment with women. Lisa, captivated by him, found the world fading away when they were together. Steven always seemed to struggle with intimacy, and for some reason, he was never fully committed to their lovemaking.

Having spent time with someone else over the last few months, Lisa's patience with Steven had been waning. In the recesses of her mind, their marriage seemed a facade and had long been over, perhaps a mere convenience. Deep down, she sensed Drake's genuine feelings, though he would never admit it. Her heart, however, belonged to someone else.

"Drake, I did not plan to stay this afternoon, although I am glad I did," Lisa said, her joy unfolding at spending an afternoon with Drake unexpectedly.

"Lisa—" he began to reply when her phone started buzzing.

"Oh, shh, it's Steven," she exclaimed after looking at the caller ID.

Amidst their connection, Steven's call interrupted, his voice reaching through the phone.

"Hello baby, how is your day going? What's up with you?" he asked.

"It's going alright," she replied as Drake lay quietly underneath her.

"I got back early and stopped by the office on the way. I was just about to leave here. I wanted to find out if we could have dinner. I should be home in about forty-five minutes?" Steven asked.

"Yes, that would be wonderful. I should be home about the same time if I leave the shop now. I just need to lock up," she responded.

"Great, I will see you soon," he said.

"Okay," Lisa mumbled.

Meanwhile, Drake was kissing her neck in an attempt to seduce her once again. She hung up the call with Steven and pushed Drake away lightly.

"You need to stop; I have to go," she giggled.

"Your mind may be telling you to leave, but your body is telling you to stay!" he said in a playful tone.

Lisa was lost in the moment in Drake's embrace. She managed to wiggle herself out of Drake's arms and started dressing and maintaining composure, all the while fearing the impending evening. The tangled web of emotions, commitments, and desires tattered, leaving Lisa at the crossroads of two conflicting worlds.

Chapter 2: A Fateful Twist

With her heart pounding fiercely and the intensity of a gambler trying to beat the house, Lisa slipped into an everlasting race against time, single-minded to reach home before her husband, Steven. The chaotic noise of honking horns and rumbling engines surrounded her as she made her way through the congested traffic, her eyes flicking anxiously between the road ahead and the clock ticking on her dashboard.

Fortunately, the geography of distance remained Lisa's steadfast ally. With a triumphant sigh of relief, she pulled into her driveway, a mere ten minutes ahead of Steven's estimated arrival. In a whirlwind of urgency, she darted inside, her pulse echoing in her ears as she dashed toward the bathroom. Once inside, she turned on the hot shower, and the water cascaded over her like a cleansing torrent, washing away not only the grime of the day but also any lingering scent of Drake. She wanted to get rid of his scent and hoped to erase it entirely from Steven's olfactory radar.

Lisa's gratitude to the heavens was discernible as she scrubbed vigorously, each droplet carrying away the potential residue of her discreet rendezvous. The bathroom allowed her to shed the layers of her deception and treachery to Steven, albeit temporarily. The steam curled around her, enveloping the purging of evidence.

As the water flushed down her body, Lisa focused on regulating her breath and senses, striving to regain composure before the impending encounter with Steven. The rhythmic patter of the shower became a soothing background to her mental efforts, aiding her in connecting with her surroundings. She listened intently, ears perked up for any signs of Steven's arrival.

In the distance, she heard the creak of the garage door, a sound that triggered anticipation and guilt. Lisa's senses heightened, and she braced herself for the approaching interaction. Time hung in suspended animation as the door swung shut, signaling Steven's return to their room.

The atmosphere in the bathroom felt charged with the approaching interaction as she worked diligently to plaster a genuine smile on her face. Deception had become her art, and in that moment, she considered herself a master, masking the complexities of her hidden world beneath a veneer of marital normalcy.

Her delicate fingers were massaging the shampoo into her hair when the bathroom door creaked open, revealing Steven's inquisitive eyes peeking through the crack.

"Hey, how is the water?" Steven's voice cut through the mist.

"Oh... it's wonderful!" she replied with a forced enthusiasm in her voice, concealing the earnestness she felt moments before. She was attempting to mask the fact that she had barely made it home in time. Steven, seemingly oblivious to her inner turmoil, pushed the door wider open.

"Don't rush on my account; I can join you," he said.

Lisa's eyes met his. She was in no mood for another physical round, and with Steven, it was out of the question right now.

"Sure, come in..." Lisa's words trailed off, and she hurriedly stepped out of the shower, droplets of water on her skin. Steven looked slightly taken aback. Suddenly, there appeared to be an unspoken tension between them as their eyes locked in a silent exchange. Steven could not blame her reluctance after all that he did to her.

Regaining his composure quickly, he said, "Oh...wow, have I told you lately how beautiful you are? I missed you, baby."

His eyes lingered on the curves of Lisa's body, admiring the curving planes of her hips and breasts. She blushed, caught off guard by the unexpected compliment, the warmth of embarrassment spreading across her cheeks. It had been ages since she had received such compliments from her husband.

"So, where do you want to have dinner?" Lisa deftly changed the subject, wrapping herself in a towel as she proceeded to dry her dripping wet hair. Steven, undiscouraged, divulged his plans for the evening.

"I found a new restaurant. It is Mexican food, but I think you will like it," he said with excitement.

Lisa forced a smile in response. "Well, I will be ready in a couple of minutes. Are you going to shower?" she asked, facing Steven through the bathroom mirror.

"Okay," Lisa said, leaving the bathroom, her wet hair trailing droplets on the floor as she moved.

Steven's eyes followed her every step, the intensity of his eyes persistent on her as the towel dropped gracefully. Her favorite dress, a flowing ensemble of deep burgundy, awaited her on the hook just inside the closet. Before putting on the dress, Lisa lathered her entire body in vanilla and peony-scented moisturizer, a scent that Steven had long associated with her. Then, she strolled over to her vanity and began massaging the cream onto her face, caressing her neck and décolletage until her skin glowed and reflected the dim lights in the room.

Her self-care routine had always been elaborate; she would slather product after product, which is why she looked much younger than her age. From the drawer of her vanity, she pulled out her blow-dryer, styling her hair until it was bouncy and luscious. Next was her makeup; she didn't need much, just some rouge and red lipstick would always do the trick.

Alas, she reached for the dress, but through the corner of her eye, she could feel Steven sneaking around, his eyes fixed on her silhouette. A playful smirk graced Lisa's lips.

She reveled in the attention, though a weak queasiness fluttered within her, a subtle warning that she chose to ignore.

"Don't you have anything to do?" she asked him teasingly.

Steven responded with a simple, "Nope, just waiting for you."

"Give me a minute then," she said as she dressed. Casting a final look on her reflection in the mirror, she adjusted her necklace.

"I am ready," she told Steven with a satisfactory glance.

Steven, immersed in his phone, his thumbs tapping the screen as if typing an urgent message, did not listen.

"Steven?" Lisa called him.

"Oh, you're ready," he smiled, raising his head. "It's the office. They keep nagging, but I just told them not to bother me tonight."

A warm smile graced Lisa's lips. Slipping his phone in his pocket, Steven walked towards her.

"After you, my love!" said Steven.

Together, they ventured towards the garage.

"Let's take my car, just something different," Lisa announced. Now, it was her turn to move a step closer to save their marriage.

Steven, who had been wanting to drive his own car, hesitated briefly but couldn't bring himself to dismiss Lisa's suggestion. Ever obliging, he accepted the change of plan with a nonchalant nod.

"Sure, I haven't driven it in a while," he said, quickly pulling out his phone to check and reply to a few messages before pocketing it.

He seized the keys from her outstretched hand, a silent agreement passing between them. The car door opened, revealing a world of possibilities within the sleek interior.

Lisa gestured gracefully, "After you, my dear."

As Steven guided the Lexus onto the open road, the purring engine became a soothing melody of horsepower beneath his fingertips. The smooth curves of the car indeed added to its elegance.

"Now I remember why you love this car. Do you want to trade?" Steven teased, his words plaiting faultlessly into the well-known banter that marked their years of matrimony.

With its magnificent exterior, the Lexus seemed almost like a third companion in their journey through life. Lisa shot him an incredulous look as if he was joking.

"Why would I want to do that? Anyway, where is the restaurant?" she asked, her eyes wandering beyond the tinted windows as Steven skillfully navigated the car, executing a swift turn onto a bustling street.

"About three blocks from the office, they opened two weeks ago. A few of the guys from the office went last week for lunch, and they said it was fantastic. I think you will love it," Steven responded enthusiastically.

Lisa observed the passing scenery with a delicate smile playing on her lips.

"And no, it's not Antonio's, but close. Just wait and see?" Steven turned his head toward Lisa, trying to read her mind.

"We'll see about that, Steven. How about some music?" Lisa suggested, shrugging off his attempt to entice her with the prospect of dinner.

"Sure. What are the options?" Steven asked. His eyes briefly scanned the road signs as he maintained a steady course.

"Well, we have the Eagles, Journey, Sade, so take your pick. Or just turn it to the jazz station?" Lisa's finger dangled between her and the radio button.

"Hmm. Let's do some old school, Sade." Steven said, pursing his lips in thought.

Lisa nodded and reached towards the car's dashboard, her fingers dancing over it to find the controls for her cherished Sade playlist. The rhythmic hum of the engine blended with the soft notes that began to fill the car's interior.

Suddenly, her focus shifted abruptly. A chilling realization struck her as she spotted a car hurtling towards the right side, where she was sitting. Panic seized her, and she instinctively grasped the dashboard.

"Steven! Watch—" her urgent warning was cut short as Steven skillfully swerved to avoid the impending collision.

"Lis—" Steven's voice faltered as the oncoming car sped through the intersection, leaving them in its chaotic wake.

He instinctively placed his hand across Lisa's chest, trying to hold her back in the seat. But the effort was to no avail.

"Steven… I am sorry, so sorry," he thought he heard her say.

The car, a sleek navy-blue BMW, blacked out from front to back, seemed to vanish into the night. Its tinted windows concealed the identity of the driver, but Lisa couldn't shake the feeling that she had encountered that ominous vehicle before.

As Steven regained control, the scene unfolded like a nightmare. The cars collided in the center of the intersection, and the world outside blurred as their vehicle spun wildly. The 360-degree motion disoriented Steven, his mind struggling to make sense of the chaos. Abruptly, their dizzying spin stopped, and their car crashed violently into the side of a massive semi parked on the other side of the intersection. The rear quarter panel caught the right side of the car, flipping it back across the intersection, eventually landing aside the fire hydrant.

The impact was jarring, and Steven's thoughts sprinted. He shrugged off the disorientation and immediately turned his attention to Lisa.

"Honey, are you alright?" his words were met only by a haunting silence.

Panic sneaked into his voice as he called out to her again, "Honey? Lisa?"

He raised his voice, trying to provoke a response from her, but she did not answer. His heart began beating faster at the continued silence from her end.

He could hear sirens wailing in the distance, growing louder as emergency responders raced towards the scene. Steven's eyes remained fixed on Lisa, who had borne the brunt of the collision on the passenger side. Desperation dawned on his face as he attempted to revive her, but the only response was the uncanny silence that surrounded him.

The seconds stretched into an agonizing eternity until, suddenly, Steven's door was wrenched open. A figure in a fire department uniform peered in. Steven's eyes struggled to focus as he met the gaze of the first responder, who was assessing him with a dissecting gaze.

"Sir, are you alright?" the fireman asked.

"I am conscious, but I think my leg is stuck. My wife is not answering me. Can you get her out first, please?" Steven's plea trembled with desperation, his eyes moving between the fireman and the twisted wreckage where Lisa lay unconscious.

The fireman nodded solemnly. His hands swiftly grasped the radio at his side, and he spoke with an urgency that mirrored the gravity of the situation.

"We have one man conscious and talking, but the passenger, the female, is unconscious. Bring a stretch and the Jaws of Life. The car is in bad shape. They are both trapped. Immediate assistance is required," he spoke.

A second fireman approached Steven. His demeanor was both authoritative and compassionate.

"Sir, I need you to stay calm. I need to put this collar on you, in case you have damage to your neck. It's for your protection. Help is coming for your wife. May I ask you some questions?" he asked Steven.

With his thoughts all jumbled up, Steven nodded in consent. His gaze flashed back to Lisa, still a haunting silhouette in the wreck. Panic clawed at his chest, but he forced himself to focus on the questions posed by the fireman.

"What is your name?" the fireman asked.

"Steven Blackman," he replied.

"Do you know where you are?" the fireman continued his questions in a bid to assess Steven's mental state.

"Yes, we're in a car accident on 5th and Woodbine," Steven responded, his eyes skimming the scene for signs of impending help.

"Thank you, Mr. Blackman, but I need you to keep still. And what day is it?"

"It's Wednesday," Steven responded, although the days of the week were a blur in the ensuing chaos.

"Good, and what is your wife's name?"

"Lisa… Lisa Blackman. Is help coming? She's badly hurt," Steven said; perseverance streaked his voice, a plea for reassurance.

He did not want to waste time on stupid questions. He wanted help to arrive fast. Lisa's deteriorating condition made blood flow faster in his veins.

"Yes, sir, they are approaching now. Please stay calm. She will be taken care of, and I am right here. I'm not going anywhere."

The fireman's words offered a fragile solace to Steven amidst the fractured moments of the accident. He nodded, endeavoring to cling to a semblance of calm as the sirens grew louder, heralding the arrival of salvation in the night.

He watched the man force the car door open so they could get Lisa out of the passenger door. As the firemen orchestrated their rescue, Steven felt the world around him warp. Time itself seemed to slow, and each passing second felt like a one-sided eternity. The gravity of the moment eclipsed everything else; priorities shifted like tectonic plates beneath his feet. Within the chaos, clarity emerged—all that mattered was Lisa's safety.

The cold touch of fear gripped Steven's heart as the firemen secured a collar around Lisa's neck. She lay there, a fragile figure in the jaws of metal, unconscious and vulnerable. A shiver ran down Steven's spine as the reality of the situation sank in.

"Sir, we are coming. Just stay calm," one of the firemen announced.

"Thank you. Please just get my wife to the hospital. I'm fine," Steven beseeched for Lisa's swift transportation to the hospital. His desperation was quite detectable at the moment.

"Yes, sir, she's on her way."

Steven watched them carry Lisa on the stretcher to the ambulance. The rhythmic thud of footsteps accompanied Lisa's departure on a stretcher. The ambulance raced away into the night, leaving Steven behind in the ruins.

A few minutes later, another fireman arrived at the driver's door. "Sir… don't get startled, but we are going to be making more noise. Do you know how we got your wife out? I am going to cover you with the blanket for protection from any sparks the same way I did with your wife," he said.

Steven nodded, confused by the words but agreeing with them.

As the fireman covered him with the protective shield, Steven's senses became more sensitive. The acrid scent of burning metal lingered in the air, and the distant wail of sirens provided a dissonant soundtrack to his predicament. Nausea took over him precariously.

During the rescue, Steven's consciousness had started to falter. Darkness crept in, eclipsing the lambent lights of the rescue operation. Silence enveloped him like a heavy cloak, leaving only the distant echo of his own breath.

"Sir, can you hear me?" the fireman's voice punctured the darkness.

Consciousness was slipping through his grasp as he floated between wakefulness and oblivion. His attempts to respond were becoming futile as well. Steven tried to answer, but the words would not come out. He formulated a response in his head nonetheless but could not replay it in sound.

"Sir, hang in there. We're almost done," the fireman repeated.

Steven tried to nod and signal that he was listening. But his state of mind refused to cooperate with him.

Lisa's Lexus lay in a crumpled pile of metal on the tow truck. The oncoming vehicle was speeding through the intersection at over 60 mph when he t-boned them. By the time Steven saw the car, it was too late.

"Sir, we need to put an IV in your arm. It's only saline and oxygen. Do you understand me?" he asked.

The ambulance driver alerted the ER when they were about 15 minutes away from the hospital. Steven could feel a rapid charge with the oxygen pulsing through his body. He started to regain some sense of consciousness. However, his only concern was Lisa.

He could hear the ambulance's siren wailing through the city, echoing off the buildings as it raced toward the emergency room. Inside, the urgency was evident. Steven lay on the stretcher with the oxygen mask clung to his face.

"My wife," he choked out.

"Sir," the paramedic replied.

"My wife… is she okay?" Steven managed to formulate the question with great difficulty.

The paramedic focused on the task at hand and responded with measured calmness, "I don't know, sir, but we are nearing the hospital, and I will find out for you."

The passing cityscape blurred outside the ambulance windows while Steven's mind journeyed back in time, retracing the steps of his life with Lisa. Their college days, filled with the naivety of youth and the promise of the future, started flashing before his eyes.

In those early years, struggling through the challenges of academia, Steven found support in Peter's friendship and the comforting presence of Lisa. The college English class, a daunting hurdle for someone not inclined toward writing, became bearable because of Lisa's natural talent with words. His mind dawdled on the moment he first laid eyes on Lisa, leaving the cafeteria with Peter by her side. Back then, they were just friends, and Steven was relieved when Peter introduced her as his friend.

Unbeknownst to Peter, his decision to move aside allowed a connection to blossom between Steven and Lisa. Her eyes drew him in from that first hello. Their relationship grew, fueled by shared dreams and implicit promises.

As the ambulance moved through traffic, the past and present collided in Steven's mind. The situation's urgency battled with the tender memories of love and companionship. He clung to the hope that, beyond the unknown awaiting him at the hospital, Lisa would be there, safe and sound. The seconds ticked away, each one bringing them closer to answers, yet the unknown pressed heavily on Steven's chest.

The shrill wail of sirens stabbed through the night as the ambulance screeched to a halt in front of the ER. The paramedics immediately rushed out and opened the rear doors to transport Steven inside.

"Sir, we are going to move you out now. Stay calm," a paramedic reassured Steven through the chaos.

Yet, the words reached Steven's ears like distant echoes. His senses were a haze, the world around him spinning in a disorienting dance.

The cold sting of metal touched his skin as the paramedics prepped him for the imminent journey into the ER. A storm of thoughts thundered in Steven's mind, but coherence eluded him. The lines between reality and delirium blurred as he struggled to grasp the situation.

"I will find out about your wife and have a nurse come in and update you on her status," another voice promised.

The gurney beneath him shifted, and two orderlies took charge, their gloved hands firm as they moved through the cold, antiseptic halls of the hospital. Steven strained to make sense of the fragmented conversations around him. Vital signs were relayed, and the details of the accident unfolded in disjointed fragments. The walls seemed to close in as he fought to remain conscious.

Breathing became a battle, each inhalation a struggle against an invisible force. The world retreated, leaving him suspended in a void where time lost its grip. Darkness descended like a heavy curtain, shrouding him in an abyss. Steven teetered on the precipice of existence at that moment, a liminal space where questions loitered like specters.

The last vestiges of awareness stuck to the distant plea of a doctor urgently calling for paddles. A rush of fear gripped Steven's fading consciousness. *Was this the end? Was he on the cusp of an irreversible departure?* In the disarray of his thoughts, he struggled with the indecision of what lay beyond the threshold of life.

Did death arrive with a burst of blinding light, or did it usher one into the quiet expanse of nothingness? The haunting contemplation reverberated through his fading senses, leaving him suspended between life and an uncertain afterlife.

Chapter 3: Echoes of the Chaos

Steven's eyes fluttered open, his consciousness slowly emerging from the depths of sleep. He first noticed the persistent sound of beeping machines and the sterilized scent of a hospital room. A dull ache pulsed through his temples as he tried to make sense of his surroundings.

"Lisa," he groaned, the name escaping his lips almost involuntarily.

He felt the need to act quickly. A whisper from his subconscious told him something was amiss. As he tried to piece together the events that led him to this foreign place, the pale morning light filtered through his hospital room's window. The dew on the leaves outside was untouched by the advancing day, mirroring the unease that tightened its grip on his heart. He squinted against the brightness as he looked around the room.

Soon, he remembered that he had spent most of the last night in and out of consciousness. However, his mind was still fighting to stay awake, trying to reconsider everything that had brought him here. And suddenly, the memory of the accident started flashing before his eyes—the screeching tires, the blinding headlights, the sickening crunch of metal.

He winced, both from the vivid recollection and the pain that pulsed through his body. The room seemed to spin for a moment before settling back into place.

Determined to shake off the fog of drowsiness, Steven attempted to swing his legs over the side of the bed. However, as he did, a jolt of pain shot through them and traveled up his spine, forcing him to gasp and retreat. A heavy sigh escaped his lips, the frustration evident in the lines on his forehead.

Just as he wrestled with the discomfort, the door to his room swung open, revealing a nurse with a clipboard in hand.

"Mr. Blackman, you are not allowed to move yet," she asserted.

Then, she busied herself checking his vitals. Her eyes flickered between the readings on the monitors and the man lying in the hospital bed.

"Fortunately," she added with a warm smile, relaxing her expression, "you did not sustain severe injuries. However, there is a slight concussion, and we will need to keep you for some days to ensure you are completely fine."

With practiced ease, she adjusted the intravenous drip connected to Steven's arm.

Steven attempted to reciprocate the smile but found his facial muscles unresponsive. There seemed to be little room for expressions of reassurance. Instead, he focused on a more vital concern.

"My wife?" he asked.

The nurse paused briefly, her eyes meeting his with empathy.

"Do you want to see her?" she asked gently.

Steven nodded vigorously. The mere thought of seeing Lisa was enough to ease his shooting pains.

"Your wife is stable enough, so you can visit her. But she is not completely out of the woods just yet," the nurse cautioned. "Do you still want to see her?"

Eager to be by Lisa's side, Steven affirmed his desire.

"Yes, please. I want to see her," he replied, with both urgency and gratitude.

With a nod, the nurse picked up the room's extension and called a male colleague.

"Michael, can you assist Mr. Blackman? He is ready to see his wife," she said.

A few moments later, a sturdy male nurse entered the room with a kind smile and approached Steven.

"Hello, Mr. Blackman. I will help you get to your wife's room," he said with genuine warmth.

Steven, though grateful for the assistance, could not ignore the elusive discomfort of dependency.

As Michael skillfully wheeled the wheelchair into position, Steven reluctantly settled into the chair. Steven felt a twinge of frustration at his inability to move on his own, but he pushed it aside, focusing on the impending reunion.

The hospital's hallways, saturated with the clinical scent of bleach and antiseptic, felt like a confining maze for Steven. As Michael took him through the corridors, he could not avoid the desire to escape the clutches of the medical facility and breathe in the freshness of the outside world. The walls seemed to close in on him, suffocating him with anxiety and uncertainty.

At last, Steven found himself in front of Lisa's room, a place that held both comfort and despair. Michael opened the door as it creaked and wheeled Steven inside, revealing the interior where Lisa lay, her once vibrant spirit overshadowed by the frailty of her unconscious form. The soft covers cradled her, but the vulnerability was evident across her face, cutting through Steven's heart.

As he eased into the room with the wheelchair squeaking softly, Steven's breath caught in his throat. The sight of Lisa, so fragile and delicate, tugged at his memories of their shared laughter, stolen glances, and the warmth of their embraces. It was as if the harsh reality of their arguments and fights had dissipated, leaving behind only the echoes of their blissful moments.

He settled his wheelchair beside Lisa's bed and asked Michael to leave them. His eyes started welling up with tears that threatened to spill over. With Michael's departure, Steven felt a flood of emotions: regret, longing, and an overwhelming sense of helplessness.

Steven found himself just sitting there, staring at her. He couldn't leave her side after whatever had happened. A single tear streamed down his face. He sat there all day despite Michael's insistence that he should go back to his room for rest. He traced the contours of her face with his eyes, mentally retracing the lines that defined the woman he loved. The hushed whispers of machines monitoring her every heartbeat provided a surreal soundtrack to his introspection.

It was around dinner time when reality snapped back into focus. Lisa's serene form convulsed; her body started shaking violently as if caught in the grip of an unseen force. Panic ran through Steven, rendering him momentarily paralyzed, unable to comprehend the sudden turn of events.

At that critical moment, the door opened, admitting a doctor clad in a white coat. With a measured tone, the doctor informed Steven that Lisa was being rushed into surgery. As the doctor spoke, the world around Steven blurred. He tried to make sense of a sudden turn of events.

"What? But why?" Steven's voice trembled with desperation and disbelief.

"The bleeding in her brain has not stopped; it was only slowed down momentarily. So now, we have to do another surgery," the doctor informed Steven, alarming all his senses.

Steven could feel the force of those words settling heavily on his shoulders, a burden he hadn't predicted. Another surgery meant more uncertainty, more risks, and an agonizing wait for the outcome.

Once the doctor left with Lisa, Steven was taken back to his room. The walls seemed to close in on him, suffocating him with his powerlessness. Nurses and medical staff moved in and out, checking on him.

Each time they entered, Steven couldn't help but ask, "How did this all happen? Has anyone found out yet?"

But the answers were always the same, offering little comfort.

Finally, the doctor returned, pausing briefly at the door. “We don’t have enough information yet, but we’re doing everything we can,” he said.

The minutes seemed to stretch into an eternity as Steven mulled over his dilemma regarding Lisa’s health. He could hardly deny that his wife’s life was suspended between the known and the unknown. However, he found a little hope in the doctor’s assurance that there would be updates on Lisa’s condition in the next few hours and a complete update within a few days.

The whole incident had left Steven utterly speechless. He never expected to see Lisa in such a state, with tubes protruding from various points on her body, connecting her to life-sustaining machines. Steven’s mind replayed the memories of their tumultuous relationship in the hushed stillness. He knew that Lisa had been unhappy in their marriage, as he failed to be emotionally and physically available to her. The overwhelming guilt consumed him, a bitter realization that he might have driven her away.

As the days wore on, the hospital transformed into a purgatory of waiting. Trapped in the confines of his thoughts, Steven struggled with the helplessness that troubled his soul. The routine of waiting for updates on Lisa's condition passed in a humdrum lull.

Amidst the quiet of despair, Steven also awaited news from the police. They had promised updates on the investigation that led to the accident. However, the silence from the authorities only added to the mounting frustration. He wanted to understand the trajectory of their investigation, to find comfort in answers that remained elusive. Yet, the door remained closed, and the corridors outside boomed with a haunting silence, leaving Steven in the throes of a disconcerting solitude.

However, the day to finally say goodbye to the hospital arrived. Brandie, his sister, was en route to pick him up. So, he decided to spend some time with Lisa before his temporary escape from the clinical walls of the hospital.

"Steven," a voice interrupted his thoughts.

He saw a nurse peeking her head through the partially open doorway.

"Yes?" he responded, restlessness gripping him.

"Are you ready to go upstairs?" the nurse asked. "We will get your paperwork ready while you are with Mrs. Blackman."

"Yes, please," he consented.

“Are there any changes in her condition?” he questioned.

“I don’t know,” the nurse answered apologetically. “But they will tell you soon, so hang in there.”

Steven wanted to convey his impatience, but given his injuries, he chose silence, nodding in acknowledgment instead. The orderly, who had accompanied the nurse to his floor, positioned Steven’s wheelchair for departure, and the trio set off toward the elevator.

“So, how are you today, Mr. Blackman?” the orderly asked, attempting small talk.

His tone was light but carried a genuine interest.

“Feeling much better,” Steven responded congenially, offering a fleeting smile. “Thanks for asking.”

The elevator journey was brief, surprising Steven with its swiftness. Memories of the seemingly endless corridors from his previous visits to Lisa contrasted sharply with the efficiency of this ascent. It puzzled Steven because the last time he visited Lisa, it took him quite a while to get there.

“Mrs. Blackman has been moved to the second floor. She is in room 206,” the orderly chimed in, observing Steven’s perplexed expression.

“Thank you,” Steven nodded in understanding. “Are you coming back to get me?”

“It may not be me, but just page a nurse, and someone will come to get you,” the orderly explained, his perpetual smile stamped across his face.

"Great, thanks," Steven replied, the anticipation evident in his voice.

The orderly exited, closing the door behind him, leaving Steven alone beside Lisa's hospital bed.

As he took in the sight of Lisa, a profound sadness welled up within him. The beeping monitors and the hushed whispers of machinery underscored the fragility of life. With each passing moment, Steven found himself suspended between hope for Lisa's recovery and the ominous specter of an unknown future.

The sight of the love of his life, connected to a labyrinth of medical instruments, stirred a deep-seated horror within Steven. His heart, heavy with regret, resonated with the disquiet of the room. The discomfort within him coiled like a serpent, making his stomach roil with unease and his nerves tingle with a deep discomfort. It was a visceral reaction, an acknowledgment of the fragility of the life that lay before him.

With a bowed head, Steven succumbed to the vulnerability of the moment. He clasped Lisa's hands in his, and with tears welling in his eyes, he began to speak, "Honey, I am so sorry for all the hell I have put you through," Steven confessed. "None of this is your fault. If I had not been so determined to be successful, you would not have spent all these years alone," he whispered.

Guilt consumed him as he continued to pour his soul into the confession.

“The occasional dinner or stage play we went to see together were measly compensations for my indifference day in and day out," he told her.

“It’s all my fault! It’s all my fault!” he added, a groveling edge overtaking his voice.

With trembling sincerity, Steven engaged in a one-sided dialogue with Lisa’s slumbering form. He bared his soul, leaving no corner of remorse unexplored. He confessed his shortcomings, the hollowness that success had brought to their relationship, and the scars of neglect that time had engraved into their shared history.

He carried on with his melancholic monologue. As if caught in the undertow of memories, Steven’s voice softened, “Do you remember our six-month anniversary? I got you those pearls that you had hinted at wanting several times. So, I made some calls and got you that set for our anniversary. I still remember the look on your face the night I gave them to you; it was priceless,” he told her.

Just when he was about to conclude one of his many confessions, his sister entered the room. Her whispered greeting startled him, and their eyes met in a silent understanding. She clasped a hand on his shoulder in a gesture of comfort.

“Don't let me interrupt,” she assured him.

“No, you aren’t,” he responded, turning his wheelchair toward her. “I knew you’d be here soon. I am just glad you could get away again today.”

Settled behind his wheelchair and mirroring Steven's concern, Brandie examined Lisa's motionless form.

"Any new updates on Lisa?" she inquired.

"Not yet," Steven replied, a shadow of gloom passing over his face. "The nurse said there has been no change."

"I hope she will be alright," Brandie said in gentle reassurance.

"Me too," Steven sighed.

"Well..." Brandie trailed off, shifting the conversation gently. "I don't mean to rush you, but Tay is waiting for us. He could only get away for a few hours."

"Sure, I understand," Steven nodded, pushing his wheelchair away from Lisa's bed.

"I am anxious to get home anyway," he admitted. "Being locked up in the hospital is driving me crazy. Besides, the food—if you can call it that—is awful. I know it's free—well, it's a part of the bill, but they could do much better."

Brandie could not help giggling at her brother's complaints.

"Steven, stop it. I don't want the nurse to kick me out of here," she said.

The lightness in her tone provided a momentary reprieve from the heaviness surrounding him.

The orderly was called to take him out of Lisa's room, wheeling him away from the place that held Lisa's silent form. Brandie stayed briefly, a silent prayer escaping her lips as she leaned down to kiss Lisa's forehead.

"God, please bless Lisa," she whispered. "I know you are in charge of life and death, but she doesn't deserve this."

With a last, pitying look at Lisa, Brandie turned away, her steps hastening to catch up with Steven and the orderly at the elevator. The elevator doors opened with a muted chime, revealing a small chamber of brushed steel and buttons that promised freedom from the clinical embrace of the hospital.

As they entered Steven's room, a nurse waited with the discharge paperwork, a stack of forms that marked the end of his temporary refuge within the hospital walls.

"Now, Mr. Blackman, please stay off that ankle as much as possible," she cautioned. "And remember, you suffered from a concussion, so things may be a little hazy. In other words, please take it easy."

While Steven scanned the papers in his hands, Brandie took a moment to ensure nothing was left behind. She checked the room carefully, ensuring that every belonging of Steven's was safely packed. The nurse continued her instructions, a steady stream of reminders and precautions.

"I understand," Steven replied with a grateful smile. "Do I sign right here?"

The nurse leaned over to guide him, her eyes tracing the lines of the document. "Yes," she affirmed, adding, "and you have a follow-up appointment next week with Doctor

Jenner. After that, you can follow up with your primary care doctor."

Steven nodded in acknowledgment, his signature becoming a series of scribbles on the dotted lines. Brandie idly tinkered with a table clock, a minor distraction to fill the anxious moments.

"I have to say this again, Mr. Blackman," the nurse began as Steven finished signing the last of the papers. "Although you have been cleared to return to work, try to take it easy for a few days."

"But what about Lisa?" he asked with concern.

"We are doing everything we can," the nurse replied. "But at this point, I don't have any answers."

After a heavy pause, Brandie spoke, "Are you okay, Steven?" she asked.

"I am okay," Steven croaked, weariness seeping into his voice. "It's just that I have never left Lisa anywhere. I know I often travel for work, but I always come back home. And now I am leaving her here."

Brandie, understanding Steven's situation, took his hand.

"She is in a place that is best for her right now. Besides, you can visit any time you want," she said soothingly.

With a resigned sigh, Steven allowed himself to be escorted to the hospital's parking area, leaving behind the discomforting haven that held uncertainty and the quiet prayers for Lisa's recovery.

Chapter 4: An Unexpected Discovery

The drive to Steven's house seemed like a slow, winding journey. Despite the bustling streets with people minding their business, Steven felt utterly alone. His perception seemed to blur the world into a secluded bubble where only three names mattered: Brandie, Tay, and himself. He felt as if he had already lost Lisa.

Even though he often traveled through these accustomed roads to the office or airport, now everything felt oddly different. The world outside the car seemed to lose significance, fading into the background as he journeyed through a personal odyssey.

Steven took a moment to recollect his thoughts as they pulled into the driveway of his house. The last time he was here, he had left for Mexico, not even bothering to tell Lisa. The regret of his behavior started bothering him. And now he could see the driveway stretched before them like a pathway with its cobblestone surface clattering beneath the tires as if heralding his long-due arrival.

As they parked, the aura of the house enveloped them. Steven's gaze swept across the grandeur of his residence. It was a big house that reflected both his success and seclusion. It was the fruit of his struggles and achievements, but nobody knew the shadows of isolation that lurked within its walls. This house, which Steven once considered a symbol of accomplishment, now felt like a self-imposed prison where his relationship with Lisa had been struggling to blossom for a long time.

Brandie and Tay helped Steven out of the car and sat him in his wheelchair. As he touched the wheels to steer, the thought of entering the house and not finding Lisa there sent a subtle chill up Steven's spine.

"Steven," Brandie's concerned tone broke the stillness as it pulled him out of his despicable thoughts, "Are you going to be alright?"

Steven's eyes met hers, lost in the depths of his contemplation. Confusion passed over his face, unsure of his sister's query.

"You know, living alone and all," Brandie said gently, being the perceptive sister she was.

Steven nodded as a sigh escaped his lips.

"Yes, I will be fine," he said.

Brandie arched a skeptical eyebrow at this response, prompting Steven to surrender another sigh.

"I promise to call if I need anything," he added.

Brandie nodded with a hint of skepticism.

"I have arranged for a nurse to stop by for the next few days. I know you have a housekeeper, but she doesn't know how to care for you in this state. As far as I know, you will not take your medicine as you should," she said concernedly.

Gratitude touched Steven's eyes as he smiled at his sister's familiar know-it-all maternal stance. Despite the irritation it often caused him, he could not help but feel grateful to his sister.

"Thank you. I will be fine," he told her with a mixture of appreciation and assurance.

However, Brandie remained undeterred.

"Alright, I will call later to check on you," she said firmly.

With one last smile exchanged, Steven wheeled himself towards the front door. Brandie observed in silence as he opened it, the cool evening breeze brushing against his face. Waving him goodbye, she and Tay pulled out of his driveway, leaving Steven alone in the quiet bubble of his thoughts.

The hallway echoed with the soft whir of his wheelchair as he entered. The creak of the front door closing reverberated, reminding him of the isolation that enveloped the house, which was once filled with the laughter of Lisa and their shared moments. But now, it held an unnerving stillness that seemed unbearable to Steven.

As Steven wearily traversed towards the kitchen, he realized that the details he had overlooked demanded his attention. Once an organized space, the counter was now scattered with accumulated mail. Yet again, Lisa's absence struck him hard.

The daunting task of going through all this now loomed over Steven like an intractable mountain. Lisa had always looked after the mail, bills, and household details. He needed not to take care of such matters in her presence. She used to manage their home effortlessly, leaving Steven free, bound only by his office duties. In her absence, the orchestra was silenced, and chaos reigned.

A heavy groan escaped him as he gathered the scattered papers, his fingertips grazing the corners of envelopes as he pulled himself together. With a makeshift bundle of papers placed on his lap, Steven wheeled his chair toward his bedroom, intending to retreat from the turmoil that awaited him.

However, as he did, his eyes fell on one carefully arranged care package in the sea of bundled envelopes. His wearied mind momentarily forgot the impending task of sorting these envelopes, focusing instead on the unexpected package.

A fleeting thought crossed his mind: perhaps the housekeeper had left it there. Overcome by his curiosity, he gingerly peeled back the layers of the package. The contents revealed themselves as an assortment of Steven's favorite snacks nestled alongside a carefully selected healthy entrée.

A tender smile crept across Steven's face as a spontaneous response to the thoughtfulness of this unassuming care package.

"This is just like her," he muttered under his breath.

The gesture mirrored Lisa's signature touch as she always thought for his well-being. But at the same time, Steven's heart ached at the thought of her being in a coma, accompanied by a realization about how much she cared for him. Would he ever be able to make up for his past mistakes?

Heaving a sigh laced with sadness, Steven entered his room. Placing the envelopes on the bed, he reached for the pair of crutches leaning against the wall—left there by the housekeeper just moments before. Balancing his weight carefully, he stood up. Indeed, the crutches had significantly improved his mobility compared to the confinements of a wheelchair. Grateful for the newfound freedom, he decided to indulge in a luxury he had longed for since his hospitalization: a long, hot shower. The sponge baths he had endured during his stay at the hospital were not quite ideal for really getting clean.

Once done having a nice bath, Steven emerged from the shower. Wrapped in a towel, he made his way to the cupboard. However, his attention was abruptly diverted by a drawer on the desk that was slightly ajar. This small detail struck him as peculiar in a house that typically gleamed with orderliness. Most drawers in the room belonged to Lisa, as he only used those in the office downstairs. Also, after the accident, both he and Lisa were in the hospital, and the house was left at the mercy of the housekeeper. He knew she could not dare to enter their bedroom, let alone open a drawer. Did Lisa leave it open in a hurry?

Compelled by curiosity, Steven approached the partially open drawer and cautiously pulled it further. It revealed a collection of neatly arranged business papers. Yet, nestled within the stack was a conspicuous manila envelope bearing "Mrs. Lisa Blackman." More intrigued, Steven could not resist the urge to check its contents.

He gingerly peeled back the folded top, initially expecting ordinary documents. However, what he discovered within the envelope sent shockwaves through him. The contents were unexpected, causing confusion in his mind.

"Who could have sent this to my wife?" Steven wondered, making sense of the alarming information before him.

Steven's trembling hands clutched an ominous letter. A sudden chill ran down his spine as he read the threats imprinted in ink. The message was typed using a vintage typewriter with ink that had faded to a dull black hue. It clearly stated the demands: *thirty-eight thousand dollars* a month to keep the information hidden. Someone was clearly blackmailing his wife. But why, the question dawdled.

One of the envelope's contents, as stated in the letter, was a key to a locker at the train depot, of all places. Lisa was expected to make the first payment by Thursday at 6 p.m., which was two days away. Steven had no idea how long this situation had been going on or what information his wife wanted to keep hidden. It was the last piece of information he expected to find after all that had happened over the past week.

Steven could only fathom one explanation: Lisa must have taken some action that led them to demand payment. Something he wasn't aware of. His wife had been hiding something from him. The instinct to seek answers bloomed within Steven, urging him to ask for help from law enforcement. Yet, an uncertainty held him back. With no knowledge of the insidious game afoot involving Lisa in its dangerous gambit, he hesitated to involve the police.

The only solution he was left with was to use his connections in the IT industry. After years in the IT industry, Steven had connections to people who did not ask questions when asked to do things on his behalf.

It's time to find out what it was all about, Steven thought.

He made a couple of calls to his former acquaintances and asked for a favor regarding the threat his wife had received. Steven was too tired to eat after receiving reassurance about finding the mastermind behind it.

After getting dressed, he ingested his pain medication and drifted into sleep on Lisa's side of the bed. A thought struck him: home had never felt so welcoming. Having spent restless nights in the hospital's cramped bed with its sterile scent of chemicals and medicine, Steven gained a fresh appreciation for the unparalleled comfort of his own space.

***

As dawn painted the sky in soft pink and orange hues, Steven's darkroom was engulfed in serene stillness. The room echoed only with his snores, indicating he had been asleep for almost sixteen uninterrupted hours. The world outside his bedroom had already marched through the morning and into the afternoon, oblivious to his prolonged repose.

The only disruption to his undisturbed sleep came with the sudden intrusion of Brandie, who was resolute to check on her brother's well-being. The screech of the door announced her presence, and she tiptoed into the room. Her eyes flitted between the peacefully sleeping Steven and the dusty rays of sunlight filtering through the partially drawn curtains.

"Steven?" she called her brother in a hushed voice near his ear, but it yielded no response.

"Steven. Wake up!" she said, escalating her efforts now.

But her sleeping brother was adamant not to respond to her. She called his name multiple times, but Steven did not stir.

After such unsuccessful attempts, Brandie resorted to persistent shaking until Steven finally acknowledged her presence. He cracked open one eye lazily to inspect his sister with confusion and lethargy.

"Ahh, it's you," he mumbled, attempting to roll over and resume his slumber.

"Steven, wake up!" Brandie insisted, her concern now evident in both her tone and the firmness of her shaking.

He succumbed to consciousness, and a drop of alarm crossed his face.

“Is something wrong?” he asked, immediately jumping to a worrisome conclusion regarding Lisa.

Brandie, however, took charge, pushing him back onto the bed.

“No, it's alright. I just came to check on you. Have you been asleep since last night?”

Her worry softened into a gentle inquiry, her eyes probing for any signs of distress.

“Yeah,” Steven replied, a yawn punctuating his words as he rubbed the sleep from his eyes. The disoriented fog of sleep began to lift as he tried to grasp the passing of time. “What time is it?”

“Well, it’s after three in the afternoon,” Brandie clipped, revealing the extent of his unconsciousness.

“What!” Steven’s exclamation echoed through the room in disbelief, and Brandie couldn’t help but chuckle at his astonished reaction.

“I guess you didn’t sleep much in the hospital,” she observed, her smile mirroring the lightness of the moment.

“That and the fact that everything there made me uncomfortable,” Steven confessed, a faint grin accompanying his words.

As the reality of the day seeped into his groggy awareness, he shifted in bed, contorting his body to alleviate the cramps that had settled during his extended rest.

"Hey, grab my phone, please, see if anyone called," Steven requested, his sudden alertness contrasting with the lingering remnants of sleep.

Brandie nodded and checked his phone.

"Yes, you have a message," she said, handing him the phone. Steven thanked her before pressing play on the voice message in his inbox.

"Mr. Blackman, we have an update on Lisa. Can you please call or come in to discuss the situation," it said.

The voice on the other end seemed formal and professional yet laced with an undertone of gravity. The mention of Lisa's name instantly transformed the room's atmosphere, and Steven's heart began to beat fast.

He was suddenly wide awake.

"It was the hospital, and they wanted me to drop by. It's about Lisa," Steven declared.

Sensing the insistence, Brandie swiftly moved towards his bed. With a gentle touch, she helped him extricate himself from the tangled sheets.

"What did they say?" Brandie asked as she assisted her brother, her eyes searching for any clues in Steven's expression.

"Nothing, they just want to speak with me," Steven replied, his mind battling with a thousand possibilities.

The unknown nature of the call fueled his imagination—was Lisa worse, better, or was there a new twist in her medical journey? The unanswered questions played like a haunting melody.

"I can't get alarmed… no… I won't get alarmed. There is nothing to worry about. Maybe she has regained her senses, or perhaps there is another treatment they want to try. I have to stay positive, right?"

Steven's words spilled out rapidly, as in a desperate attempt to convince himself as much as Brandie.

"Yes, you must remain positive," Brandie reassured him.

She tried to mask her own fears, gritty to be the pillar of strength that Steven needed in that moment.

"She has to feel positive vibes from you. I am sure everything is okay," Brandie reassured.

"Steven, I will go with you. You shouldn't be alone. After all, you just got out of the hospital yourself. She will be alright," she added upon seeing Steven so panic-stricken.

Steven acknowledged her concern with a nod. He tried to regain his calm demeanor but decided against her advice.

"Look, sis, I appreciate the concern, but I will go alone," he asserted, his tone firm yet filled with gratitude.

Brandie opened her mouth to protest, her eyes pleading with him to reconsider, but Steven cut her off with a preemptive response.

"I promise to call with an update as soon as I can. I am her husband, and she wouldn't want anyone to see her like this," he explained.

Understanding his concerns, Brandie sighed in resignation.

"Alright," she conceded, knowing there was no point arguing with his headstrong nature. "I'll see you later, but you better call me the moment you find out anything, okay?" she warned, her concern lingering even as she reluctantly accepted his decision.

"I will," Steven promised.

"Love you, and know that Tay and I are here for you. We are family, and we are all we really have," Brandie assured him as she pressed her lips on his forehead, a tender gesture of solidarity in the face of uncertainty.

Steven smiled weakly in return.

Chapter 5: A Complete Oblivion

ONE YEAR EARLIER

Inside Steven's house, Lisa reclined gracefully, draped in the opulent silk gown Steven had gifted her months ago. Her gaze locked with Peter's, who lay propped on his elbow, captivated by the allure of her radiant face. Lisa could not help kissing Peter every now and then. Amidst shared smiles and tender caresses, a profound emotion enveloped Lisa—it was her insatiable longing for Peter's presence.

It hadn't always been this way. After marrying Steven, Lisa's social life, particularly with her college friends, had almost disappeared. It wasn't until a college reunion that she reconnected with Peter. This time, though, something had shifted. While Steven went to get drinks, Lisa exchanged numbers with Peter. From there, the occasional texts turned into regular calls, and soon enough, secret meetups followed—all without Steven's knowledge.

As they spent more time together, Peter realized something he had never fully admitted to himself before: he had always been in love with Lisa long before she got married. Now, with the opportunity laid before him, he knew he would be a fool to let it slip away. And for Lisa, with Steven no longer able to satisfy her and their relationship lacking the spark it once had, being with Peter felt like the escape she had been searching for.

Amused by her desperation, Peter delicately traced the contours of her lips with his finger, gently tucking strands of her hair behind her ears. Their intertwined forms created an exhilarating display of intimacy. Over the past few months, they had missed each other desperately. Despite the apparent yearning between them, they acknowledged that it was the price that had to be paid.

In the quiet embrace of each other, they savored the moments before Peter broke the silence, expressing gratitude for Lisa's unexpected call.

"I am so glad you called, Lisa. For a minute, I could not even believe it was happening," he confessed, sealing the moment with sincerity.

"Hmm," Lisa murmured, her fingers gently caressing Peter's face. "Steven failed to satisfy me again, and it had been so long since I felt this kind of passion."

"I suppose you're enjoying me then," Peter teased, kissing her cheek.

"You just can't comprehend the ache of yearning for someone you can't always be with, Peter," Lisa confessed.

"You know, darling, this isn't by choice. If it were up to me, you would always be by my side," Peter reassured, offering comfort to Lisa.

She acknowledged the futility of dwelling on the past; what was done had been done. The looming predictability of

Steven discovering their secret added a layer of tension to their stolen moments.

"You understand, Peter, it can't be that way. Anytime soon, Steven may discover our secrets. Sometimes, his simple questions make me dubious. Dodging his questions about my outings and alone time is becoming more challenging each day," Lisa confided, concern reflecting in her eyes as she contemplated the potential fallout if Steven were to uncover her affair.

Peter's expression darkened as he looked at Lisa, struggling with the mystery of her sudden change of heart.

"Why the shift, Lisa? We were drifting apart, weren't we? You insisted we keep our distance, and I accepted it. Now, out of the blue, you want me to come over. I'm lost." His words carried a hint of anger. The intensity in his voice waned as he witnessed a solitary tear rolling down Lisa's cheek.

"There's a shared history between us, Peter. It pains me that our paths seem to lead to separate futures. It hurts me to think that we have a past but don't have a future. I can't help but imagine how beautifully our lives could have been if I had married you rather than Steven," Lisa confessed. Overwhelmed, she buried her face in Peter's chest. He enveloped her in a tight embrace, resting his chin on her head.

“I know how difficult it must be for you. I understand the struggles you’re facing,” he murmured, his fingers gently caressing her still-damp hair after the shower.

“Some things are best left in the past, Peter. Pondering them only leaves us shattered. Yet, look at us." Lisa gently pulled away, meeting Peter’s gaze. “Look at how well we have done despite life’s challenges.”

Peter felt the force of Lisa’s words. “For you, perhaps. But for me, trust shattered along with our decisions. Not that I don’t trust you, but it’s just that everything seems meaningless and temporary now that you and I are apart. It’s hard to believe in anything when you and I exist in separate worlds.”

Lisa silenced him with a hushed plea, pressing her finger to his lips. “Shush, please. Let’s not speak about it. It only brings memories and pain; we’re better off leaving them behind.”

“Alright, alright, Lisa. We won’t delve into the past,” Peter assured her, his eyes fixed on hers, “but avoiding it won’t make it disappear. We can’t keep running from each other, and you know I love you.”

Shifting gears, Peter changed the topic, his gaze softening. “Let’s talk about the enchanting sight you presented when you opened the door tonight,” he suggested, a playful smile tugging at his lips.

Lisa couldn’t help but giggle, seeking refuge in the comfort of his shirt once more. Peter, his smile widening, teased, "How long has it been since we last snuggled like this? Weeks? Months?"

Reflecting on shared memories, Lisa pondered, "Wasn't it dinner after the opera?"

Peter reminisced with a hearty laugh, "Yeah. My God! What a night that was! Do you recall how difficult it was for me to leave the house after seeing you in that black dress? All I wanted was to rip it off you and spend the entire night with you in your bedroom." He chuckled, adding, "Wasn't it Steven who suggested I take you out that night?"

Lisa, wrapped in the warmth of Peter's laughter, suddenly withdrew when his lips uttered the name "Steven."

"Alright, Peter. You need to stop mentioning Steven. I can't handle this," she declared, rising and arranging herself with a sweep of her gown. Her hair cascaded over her bare shoulders, and a deep breath steadied her resolve.

"Lisa, you say that every time, yet you're the one reaching out to me," Peter retorted.

"Peter, we have the entire night ahead. Let's not ruin it, please. This is why our encounters are rare," Lisa gently reminded him. Peter sat upright, silent. Lisa took his hand, her gaze capturing his. Though he avoided eye contact, Lisa gently lifted his chin, turning his face toward her.

"I apologize, Peter. Those words slipped out unintentionally. You understand how much we long for each other. Let's seize this moment, less talk and more—" Her voice faded as Peter gently pushed her onto the plush mattress. Lisa, with a mischievous glint, tugged at his tie, unraveling it. Her hands slid beneath his shirt, pulling it off over his head.

Lisa marveled, "Oh," at the sight of his bare chest after so long. Soon, their discarded clothes adorned the room. Lisa chuckled, aware of the effect her nakedness had on Peter, driving him to full erection and igniting a passionate response.

"Oh, baby, you are as beautiful as the day we first met. Nothing has changed." Peter pressed a gentle kiss on her tender lips, kindling a familiar desire. Lisa's fingertips felt the muscles beneath his skin, and her delicate touch rippled currents through his entire body. However, she tried to avoid making eye contact and based their connection entirely on intimacy. Peter noticed it instantly and couldn't stop himself from mentioning it.

"Lisa? Look at me."

Yet she resisted, closing her eyes in a silent struggle.

"You know how much this means to me, don't you? Please open your eyes," Peter implored again. A subtle nod from Lisa conveyed everything Peter yearned for at that moment. They kissed again, passionately and fervently.

As their lips parted, Peter spoke with a sincerity that echoed through the shared history of their lives. "We have known each other for years. Growing up together allowed us to become closer and closer. There was a bond when we first kissed, and that will never change. You know that, right?

Lisa nodded again. This shared experience with Peter evoked an unexpected surge of tears. This was exactly what she had been missing with Steven. With Peter, she felt like a little girl who could always confide in him—a girl hidden from the prying eyes of the outside world. Somehow, that night felt special. It held a unique significance, reminiscent of their initial connection—a reunion akin to their first encounter.

The following dawn kissed Lisa's awakening with warm sunbeams streaming in through the window and dancing on her naked back. She looked around, and to her surprise, she found Peter was already gone. In fact, the house was engulfed in silence. Wrapping herself in the sheets, she rose, discovering her clothes neatly placed on the chair by the nightstand. A veil of bitterness masked her, concealing the uproar within. Hoping to find Peter in the bathroom, she wandered, only to face disappointment. Turning back, she noticed a note attached to the pillow, accompanied by a solitary red rose. The fragrance of the flower filtered through the surroundings as she made her way toward it.

"Last night was magical. Thanks for calling and setting my heart ablaze. See you later," his note read.

Lisa's heart sank as she folded the note, unleashing a wave of sadness that obscured any previous emotions. In moments like these, the depth of her struggle with Steven became painfully apparent. The disparity was plain—the effortless bond she shared with Peter required no explanations or expectations, making him uniquely special. They had always shared an understanding that had been a part of their past.

True happiness seemed elusive to Lisa, both with herself and others, haunted by a past she couldn't shake. Yet she had mastered burying those haunting feelings and deflecting the taunting whispers. She braced herself for the inevitable day when her escapades would resurface, demanding acknowledgment.

***

Miles away in another city, Steven sat reflecting on the complexities of his marriage with Lisa. Their recent conversation hinted at underlying issues, but fearing the consequences, Steven desperately clung to the hope of burying those problems.
He knew that if Lisa confronted him directly, there was nothing he could do to save their marriage.

Meanwhile, in comparison to his marriage, his professional life flourished; the weekend's client meeting exceeded expectations. Jada Technology consistently delivered on career promises, and a potential promotion added urgency to maintaining stellar performance. And now, with the possibility of this promotion, the pressure to improve his stature was of the utmost importance. Despite reluctance from his boss, Steven was selected for the prestigious Special Issue Technology Team (SITT) after glowing reviews from a new client, signaling a pivotal moment in his career.

Excitement buzzed in Steven's veins as his boss revealed the imminent arrival of an express package at the hotel, promising a Monday morning announcement during the staff meeting. Eager for the unfolding events, Steven rushed to the airport, where his organized nature led him to ponder the pros and cons of the intriguing offer during his flight home.

Despite contemplating sharing the news with his wife, a remaining unease from their recent disagreement about his work made Steven hesitate. Once he was airborne, the quiet hours of the flight granted him a moment for reflection. Amidst the disturbance of recent events, he craved this respite and the chance to mull over the offer without distractions. With everything going on, Steven truly felt like he needed the time off. Getting the chance to go over his offer provided him just that.

For Steven, taking time off wasn't about idle moments but an opportunity to delve into self-reflection. Within the chaos of his thoughts, he sought clarity. The precious hours in the air allowed him to carefully dissect the offer, line by line, until Steven reached a decisive conclusion.

Checking the clock, he realized there was still half an hour until his flight touched down. Choosing to seize the moment, he opted for a brief power nap. Suddenly, turbulence jolted him awake, announcing the plane's descent. As the plane landed, a wave of dread washed over

Steven. Memories of his recent unsettling conversation with Lisa loitered, making the idea of returning home unbearable.

He didn't want to meet her, nor did he want to face her right now. Making his way out of the plane and reaching the baggage claim, he made a spontaneous decision—home wasn't on the agenda for now. A night in a hotel seemed like a better prospect—a temporary escape from facing Lisa and the emotional disorder that awaited. Yet, this choice wasn't solely motivated by his desire to avoid personal confrontation. As the group's SITT liaison, Steven wanted to be alone for the night, aiming to prepare for the morning declaration without the added stress of meeting Lisa.

The mere contemplation of it left Steven with a heavy heart. He sensed a kinship with countless other men his age, all struggling with similar challenges. The idea of blending in, feeling ordinary, and detesting that sense of normalcy overwhelmed him. Shaking off these intrusive thoughts, Steven gathered his baggage and left the airport. Hailing a taxi, he instructed the driver to take him to the nearest five-star hotel, wherever it might be.

Fatigue unexpectedly settled in when Steven arrived at the hotel, prompting him to opt for an early dinner and night's rest. The rejuvenating sleep allowed him to rise with the dawn, reaching his office just as the sun began its ascent. Despite being on a salary, Steven liked arriving before his colleagues, eager to seize the initiative for the day. Perhaps it was this dedication that led to the enticing offer from the company.

Steven's ascent to the highest levels of the company was undoubtedly proof of his solid work ethic. As the executive of his team, the well-deserved promotion marked a pivotal moment in his career at Jada Technologies.

Despite his years of dedicated service, Steven had never been in an executive leadership position until now. The promotion came with a mix of excitement and trepidation, realizing the immense responsibility that lay ahead. The prospect of doubling down on his efforts invoked both invitation and repulsion within him. Undeterred, Steven resolved to embrace the challenge, foreseeing not just success in the current role but a relentless pursuit of further promotions. Yet, the present moment couldn't completely overshadow the complex emotions swirling within him.

Another important factor that motivated Steven to embrace the company's offer eagerly was a burning desire to outshine his rival, Drake Foster, aiming to gain a decisive advantage in their enduring professional rivalry. The history of intersecting career paths and intense competition with Drake fueled Steven's willpower. The mere possibility of the offer falling into Drake's hands strengthened Steven's resolve to seize the opportunity himself. As he contemplated his promotion, thoughts of rubbing it in Drake's face danced in his mind, fueled by memories of the weasel's loathsome actions. Yet Steven approved of Drake's competence, understanding that his own deserving promotion didn't diminish his rival's skills.

Glancing at the clock, Steven prepared to face Drake, seizing the moment to pack up his belongings before their inevitable encounter.

Five minutes passed, and the creak of the front office door announced Drake's arrival. Surprisingly, he headed straight for Steven's office.

"Morning, Drake. What brings you here?" Steven greeted.

"Cut the act. Who'd you sleep with this time?" Drake questioned.

"Sleep with? What on earth are you talking about?" Steven feigned innocence.

"Don't play dumb. I got the call last night," Drake retorted.

"Well, it saves me the trouble of breaking the news. You can skip the staff meeting; I'll have your secretary take notes," Steven replied.

"Typical move, Steven. You get the credit while the rest of us do the grunt work. And, of course, we have to be politically correct, handing minorities higher-paying jobs, whether they deserve it or not," Drake accused.

"Really, Drake? Turning this into a racial issue? I can outperform you in the field with clients or manage the office staff," Steven defended.

"Steven, this is about black and white! The facts speak for themselves," Drake insisted.

"Let's lay out the undeniable fact here. Fact number one: I've earned every accolade I've gained. Hard work is ingrained in my DNA, ensuring success in every endeavor. Fact two: I work my ass off to make sure I am prepared and achieve success with every task. It sounds like you may be a little scared that a Black man is just one step ahead of you," Steven affirmed.

"Scared? Me, scared of you? Don't delude yourself, Steven. This won't slide without a fight," Drake retorted.

As the tension escalated, Steven taunted, "Give it your best shot; I want to see you try."

"There's no mere 'try.' I'll not only claim your job but much more," Drake threatened.

"What's that supposed to mean? Are you planning to get me fired? I'll believe it when I see it." Steven countered coolly.

With a cryptic warning, Drake hinted at a broader impact. "Open your eyes; it's coming soon, and believe me, it won't just be about the workplace," he declared before storming out.

Steven, recognizing the awaiting threat, stood firm. Drake's resort to racial bias was a desperate move, signaling weakness rather than strength. Steven remained resolute, aware that he had to watch his back, forestalling potential allies turning against him in the office battleground. The clash was foreseeable, but Steven was prepared for whatever Drake threw his way.

In the hushed aftermath of an intense moment, Steven took a few precious breaths to steady his nerves. As the office gradually buzzed back to life, he welcomed the arrival of the staff. Masking the residual tension, Steven adorned himself with a smile, gearing up for the impending challenge. Every so often, a colleague would poke their head into his office, offering congratulations. Obligingly, Steven feigned ignorance, playing the part of a man oblivious to his own success.

The morning board meeting unfolded seamlessly, with the entire team and upper management embracing his promotion with confidence. Steven, relieved, skillfully sidestepped any potential clash with the ambitious Drake. Knowing Drake's inexorable pursuit of his position, Steven wisely opted to steer clear of that brewing chaos.

Chapter 6: A Road to Redemption

After attending different meetings throughout the day, Steven went to his new office. His belongings had already been transferred there. As he stood in the center of his corner office, Steven couldn't help but bask in the glory of the promotion. The morning's bickering with Drake was still fresh in his mind, but as he looked out at the expansive landscape from his window, he found himself strangely indifferent. The promotion was his now, and there was nothing Drake could do to snatch it away.

Heaving a sigh of relief, Steven averted his gaze from the window and looked around his office. It was adorned with sleek Italian furnishings that felt imposing and devoid of the warmth he craved. Determined to infuse it with his essence, Steven began arranging his personal belongings. Most of the items had already found their place, but one box remained untouched, its contents a reminder of his past life.

Steven sifted through the belongings, finding consolation in the memories they evoked. Yet, the last box taunted him, urging him to confront its contents. With a blend of hesitation and longing, he finally unpacked the box.

Inside was a photograph of Lisa, her smile frozen in time. Despite the distance that had grown between them, her beauty remained unchanged. Thoughts of his faltering marriage consumed him, as the last couple of days had been a constant struggle to communicate with his wife. A simple "hello" and "good morning" constituted the entirety of their conversation.

Steven felt a pang of longing as he traced over the photograph. Despite the obstacles, his desire to reclaim her love burned fiercely. His days had become a blur of attempts at communication, each word feeling inadequate in the face of their fractured relationship.

As the elation of his promotion began to wane, another emotion poured within him, pulling him toward the image of Lisa. A knot formed in his stomach, tightening with each passing moment as he found himself unable to tear his eyes away from her picture. Her beauty radiated from the image, flooding his mind with memories of their happier days. He reminisced about the little quirks that had endeared her to him, each memory a bittersweet reminder of what they once shared.

In contrast to his past flings, Lisa's beauty always outshone them all, leaving him bewildered about how they had let their relationship dwindle over the years. What was once an unbreakable bond had devolved into a mere obligation, a façade they maintained for appearances' sake. He couldn't help but wonder how long they could continue this charade, knowing all too well the grim statistics that pointed toward their eventual separation.

Regret overpowered him, wishing he could turn back time and shake some sense into his younger self. He struggled with conflicting desires, torn between wanting to set Lisa free and realizing that he had neglected to build a family together. He knew that he shouldn't have put off having a family. Perhaps that was the missing element that could have saved their relationship from its slow deterioration, he thought to himself.

Staring at his wife's picture, Steven didn't even realize that he was sitting cross-legged on the floor, clutching Lisa's photograph like a talisman of hope. Memories flooded back, urging him to reclaim what once existed. He recognized that mending their bond required more than mere effort; it demanded a steadfast commitment. Though Lisa's love had waned, he remained steadfast in believing it could be rekindled.

Perhaps, he wondered, demonstrating the importance of familial ties would change Lisa's sentiments. Shaking off the somber thoughts, he reverently placed Lisa's picture on his desk, making a silent promise to strive for reconciliation. Then, he hastened to another board meeting, where his recent promotion loomed large. His promotion might have had additional perks; however, the only reason for that was that it came with additional responsibility. The perks were compensation corporations gave their employees for sacrificing their lives.

Little did he know that soon, the days would blur into a frenzy of meetings, occasionally punctuated by encounters with his formidable new boss, Mr. Fuller.

Their initial interaction left Steven rattled as Mr. Fuller laid bare his expectations with brutal clarity. Unfazed,

Steven resolved to meet the challenge head-on, for if there was one thing Mr. Fuller underestimated, it was Steven's resilience.

Steven could tell that Mr. Fuller's life started and ended with the organization. Steven had definitely met him before, but this was the first time that Steven had met him in the capacity of his boss. This was like seeing him in a completely different light.

Despite his initial apprehensions, Steven couldn't avoid the feeling that he would adapt to his new role. After all, others had walked this path before him, and surely others would follow. It was a cycle of growth within the company, and Steven was sure to find his place within it.

As the day's meetings concluded and tasks were checked off one by one, Steven's mind drifted to thoughts of celebration. The office party had come and gone but lacked the intimacy he craved. True celebration, for Steven, meant being surrounded by those he cherished, especially Lisa, the love of his life.

With steadfastness in his heart, Steven knew it was time to address the rift between them. He yearned to mend their relationship, to rekindle the spark that had once ignited between them. He made a silent vow to embark on the journey of winning Lisa back, knowing that every journey must begin with a single step.

As Steven plotted his grand gesture to win Lisa back, he probed into painstaking planning. Knowing Lisa's affinity for fine dining, he accurately phoned her cherished restaurant, securing reservations at their most coveted spot. Concurrently, he tasked his secretary with orchestrating a lavish bouquet delivery to enhance the ambiance.

Yet Steven sensed that these efforts alone wouldn't mend their fractured bond. Despite forestalling Lisa's gratitude, he resolved to surpass mere gestures. Recalling her aversion to wearing their wedding band, rationalized under the guise of professional necessity, he harbored doubts. While Lisa vehemently denied any impropriety, Steven couldn't shake his unease about her solo appearances.

Despite her reassurances, Steven pledged to overlook suspicions, prioritizing reconciliation above all else. He was solely focused on saving his marriage, and if that meant forgiving his wife's insolence and transgressions, he considered it done already. Once everything was sorted out, Steven pulled out the wedding band, which he kept in his inner pocket with him ever since he had it made. He had used the diamonds from Lisa's original ring to create an elegant new style.

Steven's mind wandered back to a time a couple of years ago when Lisa had floated the idea of redesigning their wedding bands. At the time, he had dismissed it as an unnecessary splurge. But now, reflecting on it, he regretted his decision. It was time to rewrite their history and pave the way for a brighter future alongside his lifelong partner.

Steven hurried home, eager to beat Lisa's return. Pulling into the driveway, he noted the empty garage and swiftly punched in the security code, slipping into the house just before Lisa's arrival. Minutes later, the familiar sound of the garage door opening and the keypad echoed through the house.

"Honey, is that you?" Steven called out with nonchalance.

"Who else would it be?" Lisa's voice dripped with exasperation as she entered the living room.

Ignoring the sarcasm, Steven plastered a smile on his face, anticipating her approach. But as she veered towards their bedroom, he blurted out the first thought that came to mind.

"I've been waiting for you!"

"Why?" Lisa asked with a hint of incredulity. "Did you get fired? Is that why you're home early?"

Steven braced himself for hostility, but her suspicions veered in a direction he hadn't expected.

"No, love," he replied, injecting a note of excitement into his voice. "It's official, actually!"

"What is?"

"My promotion!" He exclaimed with joy. "I wanted to prepare a special night to celebrate with you," Steven explained, masking his anxiety beneath a facade of enthusiasm.

He just wanted her to share in his joy.

"Oh..." Lisa's response carried a drop of suspicion. "So, why are you home early then?"

"Because I wanted to share this moment with you," Steven confessed.

He longed for her to understand his excitement. How could she not see that?

"Share what? Brag about your promotion, have a drink, and call it a night. We can do that in about two minutes. You didn't need to come home early," Lisa said, her frown deepening, casting a shadow over Steven's hopes.

Steven maintained his composure despite the comebacks forming in his mind.

"Baby, I made you a promise, and I intend to keep it. Can we start over? Please," he whispered, inching closer to her and reaching for her hands.

With a delicate touch, Lisa placed her hands in his, and as he sensed her acceptance, he leaned in to gently kiss her. Despite the forced smile on her lips, Steven knew it would all be alright eventually. He desperately needed it to be.

Drawing her close, Steven revealed the new wedding band he had crafted for her.

"This is for you, my love," he said, opening the box and turning it towards her.

The expression on Lisa's face was one of pure radiance, etching itself into Steven's memory forever.

"Steven... really? Oh my God! This is incredible!"

Lisa's surprise left him momentarily speechless.

Steven remained silent, his apprehension giving way to confusion at Lisa's overwhelmingly positive reaction. He had anticipated resistance or sarcasm, not this genuine joy.

"Well, say something," Lisa urged.

"I'm shocked. Do you truly like it?" Steven asked, a hint of concern furrowing his brow.

"Yes, Steven, it's incredible. Thank you!" Lisa exclaimed.

"I remembered a few years ago when you asked to get new wedding rings, how I blew you off and thought it was a waste of money. That was a stupid decision. So, I wanted to make it up to you," Steven confessed, reflecting on how he had brushed off her previous suggestion to upgrade their wedding rings.

"I have to admit, you redeemed yourself with this one," Lisa admitted, rewarding him with a quick peck on the cheek.

"You have no idea how relieved I am to hear you say that, Lisa. I genuinely want nothing more than to mend our relationship," Steven admitted.

"I know, but you can't blame me for being suspicious," Lisa replied, not giving a moment's thought to her own actions.

"No, you're right. I haven't been a very good husband. I suppose there's more to marriage than just providing," Steven replied, his head hanging low as he allowed himself to dwell on past mistakes, the weight of regret heavy in his heart.

"You've certainly mastered the provider role, but the romance—well, that's been lacking," Lisa remarked, her honesty cutting through the tension in the room.

Despite her earlier proclamation, she struggled to let go of the pain from the past, her wounds still raw.

"Although regret did its job, my love, move on and put those lessons to good use," she added.

Steven nodded. He understood why she said that; she was looking for change just as much as he did.

"Indeed, I see that now. It takes more than material things to make someone happy. Perhaps these feelings stem from my own experiences with my dad leaving us. My mom worked tirelessly to support us on her own…"

Steven's voice trailed off, lost in memories he hadn't visited in years. He turned back to Lisa, his eyes brimming with unspoken emotions.

"But tonight, I don't want to dwell on that," he said.

Lisa nodded understandingly, her contemplation softening as she reached for her husband's hand.

"Let's focus on the future. Tonight is special. It's about us moving forward together."

Steven nodded in agreement. "You are right. Apologies are behind us now. It's time for action. It's time to show you how I feel. I owe you that and so much more."

Lisa seemed genuinely taken by Steven's honesty. It was the first time in years that he had opened up about his childhood feelings. She found herself wondering if this was the wedge that had been driving them apart. The future excited her. The prospect of actually loving the man she was married to seemed like an alien thought.

"Thank you, Steven," Lisa mumbled. "For trusting me enough to share this with me."

The silence kept them both in a trance for several minutes. They both stared into each other's eyes and found something true in them. Lisa's heart swelled with affection as she saw the vulnerability in Steven's eyes. He smiled and embraced her with a passionate kiss. The reciprocation caught him off guard.

"Oh, baby," Steven gasped. "I did make reservations at Antonio's if you want to go, or we can just skip to dessert right here."

But before he could finish, Lisa pulled away, a playful twinkle in her eye.

"Reservations at Antonio's?" she teased, her hand resting lightly on his chest. "You're full of surprises, Steven Blackman."

Steven chuckled, his eyes shiny with amusement.

"I promise, I'm not playing games," he replied, his smile wide and genuine. "We have reservations for eight o'clock."

"You know, I would love to go upstairs, but passing up Antonio's," she winked while shaking her head.

Steven laughed.

"Tonight is all about you, my dear. Whatever you want, I'll make it happen," he said.

Lisa's heart swelled with warmth as she realized just how much Steven cared for her. For the first time in years, she saw glimpses of the man she had fallen in love with, who had swept her off her feet with his passion and zest for life.

As they stood up to leave, Lisa couldn't help but feel a surge of excitement for the future. Maybe, just maybe, this was the beginning of a new chapter for them—one filled with love, laughter, and endless possibilities.

"Shall we go then?" Steven asked, smiling.

"Yes," Lisa cooed.

With graceful patience, Lisa stayed at the driveway's end. Meanwhile, Steven maneuvered the sleek Audi A6 from its resting place in the garage. Halting the car just before her, he leaped out of the car and rushed to open the passenger door, executing a theatrical bow.

"Allow me, my lady," he quipped, adopting an exaggerated English accent.

Unable to contain her laughter, Lisa settled into the plush interior of the car. A surge of happiness encased her, like a long-lost friend returning home, and she clung to the sensation with fervor.

"Remember the last time we dined at Antonio's?"

Lisa's voice broke the silence just as Steven reclaimed his position behind the wheel.

"Our tenth anniversary," Steven replied instantly.

Lisa's astonishment was noticeable.

"You remembered?" she marveled, her eyes widening in disbelief.

"I may not always express it, but you, my love, are the wind beneath my wings," Steven confessed, his words carrying the weight of sincerity.

Blushing, Lisa averted her eyes, overwhelmed by Steven's unwavering affection. The tender way he treated her burnt a sense of euphoria, elevating her to heights she had long forgotten.

"Don't stop blushing just yet; I have more in store," Steven teased, his fingers dancing over the Bluetooth controls.

"Steven!" Lisa gasped, a hand flying to her mouth in surprise and delight as the melody of Ambrosia flooded the car's interior.

Joining in, Lisa sang along to the lyrics, her voice filling the space between them with a harmonious resonance. Caught off guard for the second time that evening, Steven listened, captivated, his heart swelling with each note.

"*We have been in love for too long to worry about tomorrow. You are the only woman I have been dreaming of*," Lisa kept singing in her beautiful voice.

For the remainder of the drive, Steven savored the dulcet tones of his wife's voice, each note a reminder of their profound love.

As Lisa stepped into the elegant restaurant, the maître d' greeted her warmly, clasping her hand.

"Mrs. Blackman, it's wonderful to see you again," he said with a smile.

She returned the gesture, a polite nod accompanying her reply.

"Thank you."

His next question about her husband made her glance towards the entrance.

"Yes, he's attending to the car," she confirmed.

"Your table is ready; would you like to wait for him?" the maître d' offered with a gracious smile.

Lisa agreed, but not before requesting a dry martini from the bar.

Another question surfaced as she settled onto a stool.

“Is Antonio working tonight?”

The maître d' assured her he was, offering to summon him if she wished to speak. Lisa declined, not wanting to disrupt the kitchen’s flow.

Sitting at the bar, Lisa watched the door, increasingly puzzled by Steven’s delay. Her concerns peaked when the bartender handed her the martini, noting Steven’s arrival.

“Thank you,” she murmured, heading towards him.

“Steven...” she called out, catching his attention.

His apology for the delay was met with a curious furrow in her brow.

“Oh, there you are,” Steven said, spotting her. “Sorry for my delay. The valet asked how I liked the car. You know, one thing led to another. He also asked why I hadn’t been in to eat lately. He was sure that he had seen you several times.”

As Steven recounted the valet’s recognition, Lisa’s mind reeled with confusion.

“That’s odd; the last time we were here was on our tenth anniversary. He must have mistaken me for someone else,” she mused, trying to dismiss it as a case of mistaken identity.

“Maybe, but he seemed very sure it was you and even recognized the car. It really is one-of-a-kind. Do you know how that could be?” Steven pressed on.

"Let's just enjoy our dinner, darling. It's a lovely evening," Lisa replied her attempt to redirect the conversation evident in her voice.

Yet, beneath her composed exterior, doubts stayed, forming a shadow over their celebratory night.

Steven nodded, his eyes reflecting agreement.

"You're absolutely right; tonight belongs to us. It must have been someone else. But let me tell you again how stunning you look," he said, a smile playing on his lips.

"Thank you, and I'm so happy we decided to come here. It's been far too long. We should make a habit of this," Lisa replied with genuine warmth, returning his smile.

Steven nodded in enthusiastic accord.

"Definitely, not just tonight."

The maître d' reappeared, ready to guide them to their table.

"Ma'am, right this way," he said, gesturing politely.

Lisa's smile widened as she followed closely behind.

"Is this table alright?" the maître d' inquired.

"Yes, it's perfect," Steven affirmed.

"Oh, Chef Antonio will be out shortly to greet you," the maître d' informed them.

Lisa shook her head lightly.

"Please don't trouble him. I'm sure he has more important matters to attend to than us," she said graciously.

"No, no, ma'am. It's perfectly fine. He specifically requested to be informed when you were seated," the maître d' insisted.

Lisa forced a smile as he nodded his head and stepped away.

"Well, it seems you've left an impression on Antonio," Steven remarked.

"It must be my magnetic personality," said Lisa, chuckling softly.

"Absolutely! I mean, you've got me under your spell for a while now, right?" Steven teased with a twinkle in his eye.

She reached out, her touch gentle as she placed her hand over his, offering reassurance.

"Tonight is about us, okay? Nothing and no one can take that away from us," Lisa affirmed.

The waiter approached, ready to take their orders promptly.

"Hello, Mr. and Mrs. Blackman. Can I start you off with a drink?"

"We're here to celebrate," Steven replied, turning to Lisa. "How about a bottle of Champagne?" he suggested, seeking her approval.

The waiter bowed courteously before heading off to fulfill their request.

In a bid to steer clear of any touchy subjects, Lisa deftly steered the conversation towards Steven's favorite topic: himself. It was her fail-safe method to sidestep any potential interrogations, a skill her husband had honed to perfection.

"So, Steven, spill the beans about the morning meeting. How did the office react to your promotion?" she prodded, watching Steven stumble over his words.

Just as he was about to answer, Lisa's phone buzzed, drawing Steven's attention.

"I thought you had turned that off for the night?" he remarked, trying to hide any annoyance in his voice.

"I'm sorry, I forgot. Turning it off right now," she replied hastily, silencing her phone with a quick flick of her thumb.

With a winning smile, she diffused his irritation, effortlessly guiding the conversation back on track.

"I reckon most folks took the news well, except for Dra—" Steven started, but Lisa cut him off.

"Dra—? What's up with Drake?" she interjected, curiosity piqued.

"Well, he stormed into the office in a rage. It seems he got wind of the promotion and wasn't too pleased. He made a scene in front of everyone, then bailed on the meeting, claiming some urgent client affair," Steven explained, shaking his head.

"Hmm, why would he be so bent out of shape over your promotion? Your track record at Jada speaks for itself," Lisa mused, mentally tallying up all the reasons Steven deserved the promotion over Drake.

"Drake thinks I am only there because I'm an African American male and the clients are not important. You—" he paused. "Are you in a hurry or something?" he prodded, noticing Lisa's distracted demeanor.

Lisa shook her head, trying to mask her unease.

"No, why do you ask?" she replied, feigning detachment.

His scrutiny intensified.

"You've checked your phone four times in the last ten minutes," he pointed out.

"It's just—it's just—a friend is going through a tough time, and I promised to be there for her. I thought she might text," Lisa explained, hoping he would buy it. "Your celebration caught me off guard."

Steven's expression relaxed, understanding dawning in his eyes.

"Fair enough. Has she texted?" he queried, his concern genuine.

She shook her head, relieved that he seemed to buy her explanation.

"Not yet. But you're right; let's focus on tonight. I'll check in with her tomorrow," she suggested, flashing a grateful smile.

"Thanks; I appreciate that," Steven replied, his tension easing.

For the rest of the evening, Lisa played the part of the devoted wife flawlessly. They laughed, talked, and held hands, painting the picture-perfect image of marital bliss. Antonio's culinary skills impressed them as always, exceeding Steven's expectations.

But the tranquility of the evening was shattered when Antonio himself appeared at the table, interrupting their meal.

"Good evening, Steven. It's a pleasure to see you again. And Lisa, how are you tonight?" he greeted them warmly.

Lisa swallowed hard, forcing a smile.

"I'm well, Antonio. And yourself?" she replied, trying to maintain composure.

His eyes twinkled with mischief.

"Very well indeed. I must say, it's been too long since you both graced us with your presence. I hope the meal meets your satisfaction," he remarked, his tone laced with subtle implication.

Lisa nodded, feeling a knot of anxiety form in her stomach.

"Yes, the meal is delightful. We'll definitely have to come more often," she assured him, Steven echoing her sentiment.

Antonio grinned, staying a moment longer before he excused himself.

"Enjoy the rest of your evening. And don't bother with dessert; I have a special treat in store for you both," he declared cryptically before disappearing into the kitchen.

As the night wore on, Lisa couldn't ignore the feeling of approaching doom. Steven seemed oblivious, but she remained on high alert. She had been at the restaurant multiple times lately, but obviously not with Steven.

Chapter 7: Breaking Apart

Lisa's phone, despite promising Peter that she wouldn't check it again for the night, kept buzzing, thwarting Steven's attempts to make the night truly romantic and special. She knew it was Peter who was calling and texting her nonstop, and her mind was in a million places all at once.

She began getting nervous and jittery, fidgeting with her wine glass and fixing her hair nonstop. Steven caught on to her erratic behavior; as careful as Lisa thought she was, it still took everything she had to not take a look at her phone in front of Steven. After all, he had planned such an amazing night for her, and all she could think about was what she would tell Peter since he had been impatiently waiting for her. Noticing the rim of her phone light up once again, she decided she needed to excuse herself to use the ladies' room.

"I think I drank too much wine," she let out a forceful laugh and scurried over to the bathroom.

Steven graciously smiled, getting up from his seat in a courteous manner until she left.

Lisa rushed inside one of the vacant stalls, locked it, and finally pulled out her phone and clicked it open. Her notification bar showed fifteen texts and several missed calls—all from Peter.

"What the hell, Peter?" she said, frustrated and shaking her head.

She anxiously scanned through her messages and decided to first listen to the voicemails before she responded.

"Where are you? I thought we were meeting tonight," Peter's tone was impatient and suspicious. "You were supposed to come over after work… What happened all of a sudden?"

She quickly checked the time on her phone and realized she had spent all fifteen minutes just reading the texts and listening to his voicemails.

Knowing Steven as well as she did, she knew how anal he could be when it came to date nights. He expected her to drop everything and be wholly present in the moment, where the two of them would just stare into each other's eyes, lost in their love for each other. But it had been eons since either of them did so for the other; this was Steven's last-ditch attempt at saving their crumbling marriage, which Lisa was well aware of.

Lisa had already taken too long in the bathroom, knowing it would raise Steven's eyebrows. So, she frantically sent a text to Peter, saying:

"I will explain later…sorry."

Barely a second had passed when her phone buzzed yet again. She let out an exasperated sigh and turned her phone off for good this time, deciding she would deal with one thing at a time. For now, that thing was Steven. Walking out of the bathroom stall, she quickly fixed her hair, touched up her makeup, and headed back outside to her table like nothing had happened.

"Everything all right?" Steven asked, carefully keeping his voice free from an accusatory inflection.

"Yes, you know how the ladies' room is always busy and never has enough bathroom stalls," Lisa replied, almost as if she had rehearsed her lines in the bathroom.

Steven could feel in his bones that something was going on that she wasn't letting him know about. "Are you sure?" he asked after a slight pause.

"Yes, dear. I'm fine," Lisa said, anxious to change the topic. "Are you ready? Did you get the cheque?"

"Don't you want to wait for our special dessert? Don't want to disappoint Antonio, now do we?" Steven replied, not in a hurry to go anywhere. "Are you sure everything is all right?"

"If I say I'm not, would you stop with the questioning?" Lisa's tone got defensive. When she realized that maybe she had snapped at him, her tone lowered.

Just as she said that, the waiter arrived with their special dessert—a decadent dish, *Macaroons Haute Couture.*

"For the lovely couple," the waiter smiled. "Courtesy of Antonio."

Lisa didn't have much of a sweet tooth, unlike Steven, who eagerly indulged in the Macaroons Haute Couture, one of Antonio's specialties. As Lisa devised ways to escape her husband's company, she smiled at him; her mind was elsewhere entirely. The night had dragged on, and the possibility of meeting Peter seemed slimmer and slimmer.

"I'm ready whenever you are," she said, observing Steven finish the last bite.

"Hmm," he said as he gulped it down, wiping his face with a napkin. "Ready," he confirmed as he rose.

Lisa took Steven's arm, and the two walked back outside as her stilettos clicked and clattered on the pavement.

"I'll tell the valet to fetch our car," Steven gently let go of Lisa's arm and walked ahead of her.

Lisa seized this moment of distraction from Steven to send a hurried update to Peter, whose messages were unrelenting.

"I'll try to slip away, but don't count on it," she messaged.

"What? Just tell him you're leaving—how hard can it be?" Peter replied promptly, his eagerness observable.

Lisa vacillated between her decision to stay with Steven or to meet Peter. It wasn't as if the choice was hard; she would choose Peter over her husband any day. However, the act of escaping itself seemed nearly impossible.

"I'll try, but no promises," she responded, attempting to placate him.

"Fine!" Peter's terse reply hinted at his frustration.

"Please don't be mad. I didn't plan on this happening!" Lisa replied, trying to salvage the situation.

"You manage to get away when YOU want something!" she felt his bitterness through the phone screen.

Feeling torn, Lisa considered Peter's accusation. He wasn't wrong; she had manipulated situations before to see him. Yet, extricating herself from Steven's company tonight seemed daunting.

"Okay, okay, don't be angry. I'll figure out a way. Give me some time," Lisa had decided; she would see Peter, and not even her husband would get in her way.

As their car arrived, Steven held the door open for her, "Your chariot is here. Ready to head home?"

"Yes, I am," Lisa replied, masking her frustration with a smile.

Steven then sat down in the car, and the two drove away.

"I've been looking forward to continuing what we started before dinner. It's been too long, and I think it's a good place to start if we're going to work things out," Steven remarked, his eyes fixed on the road ahead and his hand reaching out to caress Lisa's inner thigh.

Lisa forced a smile, knowing that the lovemaking that awaited her was far from exciting.

"I agree, but do you mind if I quickly go over and check on Ashley when we get home? I'm worried about her," she requested, hoping to plant the seed for her escape.

Steven sighed, “Do you have to? Tonight?”

“I’m afraid it’s rather urgent....” Lisa skittishly replied.

Glancing out the window before acquiescing, Steven responded, “If you must, Lisa.”

Secretly relieved but trying to conceal it, Lisa leaned over and kissed Steven on the cheek. “Thank you, honey. I love you.”

“Yeah, when it suits you,” Steven muttered, his bitterness evident as he sped the car.

Confident she had succeeded, Lisa baited Steven further. “What the hell is that supposed to mean?”

Their ensuing argument set the tone for the tense drive, the fallout stifling any further conversation. The rest of the drive was spent in silence, which Lisa much preferred.

Finally, when they reached home, Lisa sprang out of the car before it fully even stopped in the driveway, grabbed her overnight bag, and scurried out of the house—all before Steven even parked. Without so much as a goodbye, she sat in her car, prepared to drive off. But first, she hurriedly initiated a call to Peter.

“Hello, are you on your way?” Peter’s voice rushed through the line.

“Yes, but Peter, you know how unpredictable things can be," Lisa replied with irritation. “I’m married to Steven. We’ve been through this. I can’t sneak out all of a sudden every time. You need to understand that," Lisa's helplessness resonated in her voice.

"Look, Lisa, I'm really sorry, but there's something urgent I have to tell you," Peter pressed.

"Look, I'll be there soon, but this better be important," Lisa snapped before ending the call abruptly.

Guilt and doubt took over her as she cruised to Peter's. Steven had put effort into making their evening special, trying to mend their relationship. Despite her hindrances with him, she couldn't deny the history they had in common. Did she truly want to shut herself off from the possibility of love?

"I can't keep this up. I have to tell Peter. This is it," Lisa resolved through tearful sobs, fortifying herself for the difficult conversation ahead.

Meanwhile, Peter waited anxiously for Lisa's arrival when his phone rang, interrupting his thoughts.

"I knew she'd do this," Peter muttered before answering, thinking that she would come up with an excuse to cancel on him.

"God, what is it now?" he asked.

As Steven's voice emanated from the other end, Peter tensed, momentarily caught off guard. "Peter, what's going on?"

"Oh...*Steven.* Sorry, I've just been getting a lot of telemarketers calling. You know how they can be," Peter said, cooking up a defense.

"Peter, I need to talk to you. It's urgent. I'll be there in about 10 minutes."

"Now? It's kind of late, and I have an early day tomorrow," Peter protested, feeling like something was amiss.

"It's important. I need your advice. Please, Peter, it can't wait," Steven urged.

Reluctantly, Peter agreed, making excuses about needing to tidy up before Steven's arrival.

As he ended the call, Peter's mind began to swirl with all kinds of possibilities. "I-I need to warn Lisa," he realized, quickly dialing her number.

"Peter, what is it? I'm already at your place," Lisa had nearly pulled up to his house but was saved in the nick of time.

"I'll open the garage. Get in quickly. Steven called me. He's on his way," Peter instructed urgently.

Lisa's face contorted in horror, "What do you mean? Is this some kind of game?" Lisa's shock was clear. But she carefully parked her car in his garage, still on the phone with him.

"No, listen to me! He just called out of the blue and wanted to come over. There's no time to waste. Stay in the garage, and I'll close it," Peter reassured, trying to keep Lisa calm.

Her voice shook, and she panicked, "He knows, Peter. He knows!" Lisa's fear and anxiety were evident in her rapid breaths. Apprehension took over Lisa, who reversed out of Peter's driveway, leaving him bewildered as he looked on from his window.

"Lisa, where are you going?" Peter's nerves were about to get the best of him.

"No…I can't do this. He knows, Peter. I can't face him tonight," Lisa seemed to be on the edge of a breakdown.

Peter tried convincing her to come back, "He doesn't know anything. Just come back and pull into the garage. Hello? Hello!"

Peter's words fell on deaf ears as Lisa disconnected the call and sped away.

Moments later, Steven arrived at Peter's house, his car pulling into the driveway. He thought he had seen a glimpse of a car that looked a little too familiar, but he couldn't be sure. He parked the car and found Peter standing right at the door. "Peter, was that Lisa's car I saw leaving?" Steven inquired as he locked his car.

"Uh, where?" Peter feigned innocence, attempting to mask his nervousness.

"I thought I saw her car leaving just now," Steven reiterated, pointing towards the garage.

"N-no, Lisa hasn't been here," Peter deflected, eager to change the subject.

Steven scrutinized Peter, "I know my wife's car, Peter."

"Maybe you thought you saw it. She's probably at home," Peter lied, attempting to maintain composure.

"That's actually why I'm here," Steven interjected. "Can we talk inside? It's getting chilly."

"Sure, come on in. You can park your car in the garage if you want," Peter offered.

"Oh no, it's fine," Steven declined.

Once settled inside, Peter expressed his concern for his friend. "So, Steven, what's going on? It's awfully late. Is everything okay?"

"Yes, I know the time . . . I just need to talk to you. Isn't that what friends are for, or are you too busy?" Steven's tone was strained.

Peter gestured for Steven to have a seat. "What can I get you to drink?"

"Nothing, I just need to get some things off my chest," Steven said, looking Peter dead in the eyes.

As Steven hesitated, Peter noticed his friend's unease. "Steven, what's on your mind?"

Steven finally spoke, his voice heavy with guilt. "Peter, I messed up. I don't know if Lisa will ever forgive me."

Peter simply stared on, waiting for Steven to finish.

Taken aback, Steven went back and forth between telling Peter, "I don't know how to say this," he whispered, scratching his jaw and smacking his lips. "After my promotion announcement, I wanted to celebrate. I got a new wedding band made, and Lisa and I went to Antonio's for dinner. She seemed happy, but I felt as if…she didn't want to…you know."

"Have sex?" Peter interjected bluntly.

"No, make love. She's my wife," Steven corrected him.

"Sure, if you say so," Peter remarked skeptically.

"What's that supposed to mean?" Steven bristled, feeling offended.

"Steven, let's face it. Romance isn't your forte. I was surprised a guy like you managed to land a woman like Lisa," Peter remarked with brutal honesty.

Steven was taken aback by Peter's 'honesty.' "I came here for support. I thought I could count on you."

Peter remained silent, lacking a suitable response. He looked down at the floor, unsure of what to say next.

Steven and Peter's friendship had deep roots, forged during their high school years. Steven's troubled past, marked by his father's abandonment and his mother's struggles, had left him totally isolated until he met Peter. Their bond strengthened when they stood together against bullies during their freshman year, making them quite popular among their peers. They became inseparable, their friendship seemingly unbreakable, at least on the surface.

After high school, Steven and Peter attended the same university, where Lisa later joined them. Though Steven had always admired Lisa, it wasn't until their college years that he fell deeply in love with her. Despite initial hesitations from Lisa's end, Steven's persistent affection eventually won her over.

Their relationship never went past kissing, as Steven believed in waiting until marriage. He viewed Lisa as his everything, seeing qualities she often failed to recognize in herself. Peter, witnessing Steven's unwavering devotion, stepped back, prioritizing their friendship above all else.

Over two decades passed, and their bond endured through life's ups and downs. Steven trusted Peter blindly, confiding in him even during the most challenging times in his marriage.

"Steve, for the past twelve years, you've provided for Lisa admirably. But you've overlooked her emotional needs," Peter gently confronted his friend. "Marriage isn't just about material provision; it's about understanding, romance, and security. Lisa needs to feel cherished and valued, not just financially supported. Maybe she feels neglected because you've been absent emotionally, spending more time at work than with her."

Peter's insight struck a chord that Steven had long ignored. Steven sat in silence, digesting Peter's words. "I'm not sure if I can fix this, especially if everything you're saying is true," he admitted, his voice heavy with regret.

"You need to evaluate your marriage and decide what steps to take," Peter advised, offering his support with a comforting pat on Steven's back.

"Should I just let her go?" Steven asked, his helplessness brimming in his eyes.

"Maybe she's already gone," Peter suggested with irony.

Steven sighed; his friend had told him a harsh truth, but maybe it was what he needed to hear. "Thanks for the advice, Peter. You've always been a good friend. Sorry I ruined your evening," Steven said, expressing appreciation before preparing to leave.

Peter hugged his friend with sincerity. "Anytime. It may feel like the end now, but things will get better. They always do."

"I know... thanks again, Peter," Steven replied as he left, his mind set on resolving the disorder within his marriage.

"Now, go home and get some shut-eye," Peter smiled at Steven. "Tomorrow's a new day, and now isn't the time to start slacking on the job. You're the man now!"

With a chuckle, Steven nodded at Peter, walking to his car. Peter and Steven waved goodbye to each other, and Steven waited for Peter to go back inside.

Sitting in his car, Steven glared at Peter's house with an incomprehensible expression. "I've had just about enough…everyone thinks I'm an idiot. I'll find the truth…if not now, soon."

His eyes fixed on Peter's house, Steven drove away in the stillness of the night, venom bubbling within him.

Chapter 8: Reality is an Illusion

As Lisa's car glided into the expansive driveway of a five-star hotel, she exhaled a sigh of relief, feeling as though she had finally escaped the confines of her everyday life. It was the ideal place for her to collect her thoughts and find comfort in the quiet. The empty roads around the hotel exuded a sense of remoteness she had long sought.

"Nobody here will know who I am. Time to unwind," she sighed with relief after parking her car.

She then scrolled through her phone, checking her notifications. Peter had been blowing up her phone as usual, yet there was nothing from Steven.

"Why can't he just call?" she muttered to herself, her mind eddying with thoughts of Steven and Peter. "I bet he's still with Peter, even after knowing everything. I can't waste my energy arguing with him."

Resolute in her decision to disconnect from the chaos, she deleted Peter's messages without a second glance, determined to focus on the present moment.

Stepping out of her car, Lisa took a moment to compose herself, smoothing down her hair and adjusting her makeup in the tinted car window. Satisfied with her appearance, she made her way towards the hotel entrance, where the scent of wild roses greeted her with open arms.

Inside the lobby, Lisa was greeted by the warm smile of the concierge. "Welcome to the Rodale! How may I help you, ma'am? Do you need me to collect your bags?"

"No, that won't be necessary. I'm only here for a quick drink," she smiled politely.

"Certainly, ma'am. Please take the elevator to the top floor; the restaurant will be right as you exit. The kitchen is closed, but the view will surely fill up your senses."

"That'll be all. Thank you!"

With a nod of understanding, the concierge directed her toward the elevators, guiding her to the top floor.

Lisa stepped inside as the elevator doors slid open, her reflection staring back at her from the mirrored walls. She couldn't help but feel a sense of satisfaction as she admired her appearance, feeling empowered by freedom.

Joining her in the elevator were a young couple; their laughter and affectionate gestures were a reminder of Lisa's own past. Watching them hold hands and kiss, she felt a twinge of nostalgia, memories of her early years with Steven flooding back to her. Her expression faded a bit as she temporarily got lost in the sea of remembrances.

When the elevator stopped and the ding alerted Lisa, the young couple bid a fond farewell to her.

"Have a good night!" the woman wished her.

"You two as well. You look great together," Lisa called after them, a wistful smile playing on her lips.

The couple, however, was so enamored in each other that they didn't even hear what Lisa said.

Stepping out into the lively atmosphere of the rooftop bar, the pulsating beat of R&B music filled the air, mingling with the lively chatter of patrons as they danced and mingled around the bar. Lisa scanned the crowd, searching for a familiar face amidst the sea of strangers, but came up empty-handed. On the other side of the roof, many tourists gathered to watch a game on a big screen, which Lisa didn't care for much either.

Undeterred, she found herself a seat near the railing and motioned to the bartender. The bartender approached her with a friendly smile as he awaited her order.

"Good evening, and welcome to the Cha-Cha Bar. What can I get for you?" he asked. His heavy accent caught her attention, and despite his youth, she could hear the maturity in his voice.

"Surprise me," she told the waiter, feeling rather experimental tonight, to which the bartender graciously nodded.

As the bartender turned to prepare her drink, Lisa reveled in the sights and sounds around her as the scent of alcohol reached her. Tonight was about more than just a quick drink—it was a chance for her to escape the pressures of everyday life and embrace the freedom that awaited her, at least for a short time.

The city skyline expanded before her like a network of glittering lights, casting a mesmerizing glow against the night sky. A slight breeze carried the smell of distant laughter and rain, mingling with the subtle aroma of alcohol coming from the bar. The calm that surrounded her, like a reassuring hug in the middle of the commotion below, was something she was unable to escape.

Within minutes, her drink was placed in front of her on the tabletop. Startled, Lisa lifted her head to thank the bartender, only to find herself face to face with someone familiar yet whom she did not expect to see.

"Drake Foster?" she called out. "What on earth are you doing here?" Gazing at the man in front of her, Lisa's voice was a mix of surprise and curiosity. Drake was always a head-turner; he exuded a handsomeness that attracted attention wherever he went. With his chiseled face, piercing eyes, and confident smile, he emanated charm and sophistication.

Drake, his expression calm and composed, simply raised an eyebrow in response. "I come here often," he explained, his tone casual yet enigmatic. "It's a nice, quiet place and not too far from my home. The question should be, what are you doing here, Mrs. Steven Blackman, all by yourself?"

Lisa's heart skipped a beat at the mention of Steven. "I'm not here to answer any questions," she replied, her voice tinged with a hint of defensiveness. "Just to relax and take in the city sights."

Drake's gaze held hers with quiet intensity as if searching for answers hidden beneath the surface. "You chose the right place, as you can see," he remarked, gesturing towards the surreal view of the city. "The restaurant circles the city, as I am sure you noticed. So, where is Mr. Blackman?"

Lisa hesitated, unsure how much to reveal to this unexpected acquaintance. "Um …he's meeting me here. He should be here any time," she replied, her words carefully measured.

Sensing her discomfort, Drake offered a reassuring smile. "Do you mind if I give you company until he arrives? Or at least till your drink is finished," he suggested, his voice gentle yet persistent.

Lisa's gaze then darted nervously around the rooftop bar, her mind racing with conflicting thoughts. She was torn between the desire for solitude and the persistent and somewhat alluring presence of Drake Foster, whose unwavering insistence threatened to disrupt her carefully sought-after moment of peace.

Steven's noticeable absence bothered her, making her feel more disturbed than she wanted to allow. However, amid her inner struggle, she found herself dealing with Drake's courteous but persistent advances.

"That is very kind of you to offer," Lisa began, being polite but not mincing her words. "But I don't think that will be very…*appropriate*. Besides, I just want to relax and, as you have already said, enjoy the beautiful city sights."

She looked at him, trying to read his expression. She thought he wouldn't take the rejection well, but to her surprise, Drake Foster was the epitome of coolness. His expression was devoid of any trace of irritation.

"I promise not to interrupt your relaxation." He began, refusing to back down. Lisa schooled her expression, trying to remain polite in the face of constant insistence. "And with you having the best table in the place…."

With her doubts growing, Lisa found it difficult to keep up her gracious exterior when confronted with Drake's unflinching insistence.

"Mr. Foster," she ventured, impatience showing in her voice. Caught off guard by his unexpected offer, Lisa hesitated for a moment before nodding. "I suppose that would be fine," she conceded, her interest somewhat piqued by him.

"I just want to know more about you," Drake's tone was humbled. "I apologize for intruding on your meeting like this, but I couldn't resist the chance to see you and speak to you."

Lisa was reluctant to give in to Drake's persistent pressure, but she couldn't help but be drawn in by the mysterious person sitting across from her.

As the moments stretched on, Lisa found herself ensnared in Drake's steady gaze, her thoughts twirling in vagueness and doubt. She had no idea she was a mere pawn and that Drake had a trick up his sleeve. He had a grudge to settle and had just set the stage for his grand scheme. Drake Foster wasn't the type to shy away from a chance given to him on a plate. What better way for Drake to rock Steven's world than by baiting him with his wife?

Deep down, he knew this was his chance to get revenge and that Steven was not coming to see Lisa. He took a seat in the chair across from her and continued to argue his point. To his astonishment, though, Lisa put up very little fight this time. On the other hand, Drake kept a straight expression. He was a master at controlling his emotions, always trying to keep his thoughts and feelings to himself.

Lisa watched Drake take in a breath, anxiously waiting for him to finish what he had sat down to tell her.

"You know, I've been with the company for over 15 years." With his hand tucked under his chin and his elbow propped up on the table, he began telling his well-crafted story to Lisa. "You may question why I'm not married. The truth is, I'm the one responsible for my divorce. I was so focused on my career and where I wanted to go within the organization that I guess I just lost sight."

He paused and looked out to the city view, his eyes distant as if reliving old memories. Only he knew whether his emotions were genuine or mere acts.

Lisa listened carefully, not wanting to interrupt Drake as he went on. "I didn't pay attention to anything else around me until it was too late. But that's alright with me. I was willing to follow that road at the time, and I can't go back and undo the choices I took in the past." With a shy smile, he turned to face her.

With a sense of empathy and curiosity, Lisa probed further, her head tilting as she traced the rim of her glass. "Don't you miss not having a family?"

"Sometimes, but I still see my children and do what every man should do. I could never let another man take on my responsibilities," he said with resolution.

"And attending places like these…is it enough to fill the void?" Lisa asked, her eyes locked with Drake's.

"Every circumstance has advantages and downsides. I don't like to show off, either. It's fun to…be myself. I have the last say when choosing a business. I travel where and when I want to. My private life is separate from my professional life, so nobody can say anything negative about me."

With his arms folded across his chest, Drake reclined in his chair. His eyes trailed the route Lisa was tracing with a delicate touch of her palm, following her finger movements. He observed her as she raised her glass to her lips and quickly sipped the contents. Despite routing the conversation herself, Lisa's shoulders slumped at the intimate nature of the exchange. With a gesture toward the waiter, Drake pointed to the empty glass on the table.

"You're not wrong, I guess," Lisa told him. "Just very different from me…" her words trailed off.

"My kids…they're the light of my life…they make it all worth it," he smiled. "What about you; do you not want children?"

Drake had struck a nerve; Lisa coiled instantly at his probing question.

"I..." she began. "It's complicated." Her words hung in the air as she glanced at the city lights.

"One day…things will change," Drake leaned in. "You'll be a great mother. Some women just have that desire and passion, and you have it." Drake offered comforting words that he knew Lisa would gobble up for self-satisfaction.

"I'm not sure if Steven even wants kids. We used to discuss it, but it would always end up in a fight," Lisa's eyes drooped as she spoke. "Although his priorities aren't quite there yet, I think that he does. But I wonder if he would have any time at all to spend with his kids." Lisa grumbled, giving in to her feelings.

"Well, I guess I got kind of stuck too..." Steven sighed. "But I have two adorable kids, so I don't mind. They pay a price, but I also know they understand."

Drake jerked to a stop and straightened his chair. "Please pardon me for a moment. I have to go use the restroom."

He quickly slid out of his chair and headed toward the bathroom without waiting for Lisa's approval. A rush of clashing emotions engulfed Lisa as she downed yet another refilled drink. Their conversation hung heavily in the air like a dense fog, leaving her feeling slightly disoriented. She was so engrossed in her imagination that she didn't realize Drake had returned until he was sitting opposite her again. She gasped as she was startled by his presence and abruptly brought back to reality.

"I'm sorry, but I wanted to ensure you were alright before I left. I don't live far from here, and we've both had a lot to drink. I booked you a room since you live on the other side of town," Drake firmly placed his hands on the table.

Letting out an exasperated sigh, Lisa exclaimed, "Ugh… no, Drake, I need to get home. You shouldn't have, really. Steven will be worried if I don't come home."

Raising his eyebrows, Drake noticed that Steven had no idea his wife was there. "I thought you said he was meeting you here."

Realizing she had fumbled, she aimed to correct herself, "Well, I uh—"

Drake chose his words very carefully, "Look, I thought Steven would feel better knowing that you are safe instead of driving under the influence and, God forbid, getting into a highway accident. I may not like Steven, but I would want him to do the same for me."

Lisa sat there, weighing her limited choices. "I appreciate your concern, and I am sure your heart is in the right place, but I will be okay with that. Trust me."

Drake pursed his lips, “What a shame. The room’s on me, and I already ordered a bottle of wine for you. You said you were out to relax, and…you should do just that. Tomorrow has its own problems.”

There was some appeal in his words, even if Lisa didn’t want to believe it. “Maybe you’re right, but my husband …”

Drake, it seemed, was quite the smooth-talker and knew how to get his way with people. “At the very least, you will go to the room, and I will make sure you are safe. After that, you can leave if you like, but I will know I have done my part.”

“Okay…okay, I will stay the night,” Lisa conceded. “Maybe I should just take advantage of my night out.”

Rubbing his hands together, Drake had finally gotten what he wanted. “Fantastic! I have truly enjoyed learning more about you. You are a remarkable woman.”

Lisa blushed slightly, enamored by his charisma. Steven, however, stayed at the back of her mind. “You can never tell Steven you got me a room, and I stayed here. You have to swear to me.”

“Why would I do that?” Drake mused as his hand caressed her arm.

Lisa felt comforted by Drake’s hand brushing against her. It brought back a feeling of intimacy that had been absent for quite some time.

“Thank you! You were right, you know,” she said.

"Right? About?" Drake looked at her from top to bottom.

"You're not like how I thought you were. I am thankful we ran into one another."

Drake could tell everything was going according to plan; he was aware that he needed to be mindful of his future moves.

"Although I know I shouldn't," he began, "I have to admit that I've had fun with you tonight. And this view is…breath-taking. You are much different than expected, and I understand now why you are who you are. Life is always through the eyes of that person who is looking at it."

Chapter 9: Crossed Lines

Lisa and Drake's conversation veered from profound to small talk. The night was still young for them, even though they were past the point of burning the midnight oil. Although the room was arranged for them before they made their way down, Lisa subtly shifted the conversation toward Peter, revealing that he was more than just a friend and had a much more special place in her life.

Drake noticed that Lisa was beginning to trust him now that she was sharing personal stories. This newfound knowledge could be advantageous for him, he thought, and he filed it away in his mind.

"Well, would you look at the time? It's getting late," Lisa remarked, rising gracefully from her seat, slightly stumbling. "Thank you for the wonderful evening."

"I should be the one thanking you, Lisa," Drake responded, his eyes reflecting sincerity. "I'm grateful you let me see a side of you that I guess many people don't get to see."

"Tonight was a refreshing escape. It allowed me to just be me," Lisa said, her smile widening.

With a grin, Drake offered to walk Lisa to her room. "Come on. The room's ready for you."

"No, no, I shouldn't," Lisa mumbled.

“I thought we were over this,” Drake said, slightly irritated. “I wouldn’t be able to forgive myself if I let you go and something happened to you.”

Lisa hesitated for a moment but then nodded.

“Okay, I’ll stay. Just promise me you won’t tell Steven about this.”

“Mum’s the word,” Drake reassured her, spreading his arms as if making an oath.

Drake paid the tab, and the two of them made their way to the elevator, with Lisa holding Drake’s forearm. Her thoughts momentarily drifted to the young couple she rode with earlier and how their evening had panned out. It made her long for a love of her own, considering her marriage was a dying flame.

Inside the elevator, the atmosphere grew thick with tension. Lisa felt an overwhelming desire to lean in, give in to her carnal desires, and kiss Drake. But how could she? Did she want to be unfaithful to both Peter and Steven and get tangled in this mess? Did she want to get in bed with her husband’s biggest threat and competition?

No.

She couldn’t. She decided against it, resisting the urge with every cell of her body. Maybe it was the alcohol talking or the fact that Drake was tall and tender, and all she wanted tonight was to be desired and have an unforgettable night. Throwing caution out the window, Lisa, in a moment of weakness, gazed into Drake's eyes, whose own reflected a mischief that could hardly be denied.

He turned to look at her, inching closer and closer. She didn't oppose his advances when he finally grabbed her hand and drew her in, their bodies touching sensuously. She stopped trying to hold back and gave in to her desires, and the two began kissing passionately, not hearing the ding of the elevator as its doors flung open.

Their embrace allowed them to get completely absorbed in one another. They had reached the wrong floor, and amid their heated encounter, they were interrupted by a couple waiting for them to get off. The man cleared his throat, raining on Lisa and Drake's parade.

"Uh, sorry..." Lisa apologized, embarrassed.

She quickly fixed her hair and straightened her dress, and Drake awkwardly smiled at the couple.

"Wrong floor..." he giggled.

He signaled for Lisa to scooch and reselected the correct floor, with the other couple waiting beside them. They finally got off, and when the doors opened, Drake hastily grabbed Lisa, scooching past the couple and into their suite.

Upon entering the room, Drake took a moment to inspect everything. He then poured wine into one glass, handing it to Lisa with a slight smile.

"Little nightcap. Enjoy the rest of the night."

Lisa looked into his eyes, her voice slightly shaky.

"Would you mind having a glass with me?"

"Lisa... I don't want you to get the wrong idea or think that I orchestrated all of this to lower your inhibitions," Drake said, hesitating briefly.

"Drake… I want you to stay," Lisa softly admitted, her eyes meeting his. "You were talking about how much I had to drink... If my memory serves me right, you had just as many drinks. Besides, I can't drink all this wine."

Understanding the force of her invitation, Drake poured himself some wine. "Alright, but we should be careful," he warned with a wry smile.

As dawn broke, Lisa stirred awake to find Drake's side of the bed empty. A tray of breakfast, accompanied by a handwritten note, awaited her on the table.

"Good morning, Lisa. I hope last night offered you the relaxation and escape you needed. It was a surprise for both of us. Please let me know if you're alright. – Drake"

Lisa's lips curled into a contented smile as she read the note. Then, her smile widened as she picked up her phone to text him a heartfelt message:

"Thank you for everything."

***

The house was filled with a weird silence as Steven awoke on the couch, too exhausted to make it to his own bed. Although his late-night meeting had granted him extra rest, his body still protested. While he sipped his second cup of coffee, his alarm interrupted the silence, and he grumbled as he made his way to the bedroom. He wondered why he needed such a sprawling house with just Lisa and himself in it.

Entering the room, Steven tried to be quiet, hoping not to disturb his wife, whom he thought was peacefully sleeping, tucked in their bed. To his surprise, the place was completely untouched, just as it had been the day before.

“She didn’t come home," he said aloud, more disappointed than surprised.

Reality hit him like a ton of bricks: it was time for a change, a change in his favor.

The room seemed to reflect his wilting marriage and life. The morning rays of the sun formed a glow on a framed photo of when he proposed to Lisa, and his eyes settled on it in remembrance. What was once a cherished memory now felt like a painful relic of the past. Without hesitation, he knocked it off the wall, not caring about the sound of breaking glass.

Today, he thought, was the beginning of a new era—the day when he would start in his new position. He had a meeting with his boss that day, but deep down, he knew escaping to work wouldn’t solve his marital problems. Maybe his work was the root of all the problems to begin with.

His mind raced with plans for a brighter future, focusing on success rather than his failing marriage. Walking across the hardwood floor, he felt a twisted satisfaction as the broken glass crunched beneath his feet. It was as if destroying these reminders could erase the love he once felt. Yet, the shattered image would haunt him forever.

Shedding away the chaos of the morning, Steven headed to the office, prepared for the day that awaited him.

"Good morning, Mr. Blackman," greeted Sarah, his secretary, as he entered his office.

"Morning, Sarah. How are you?" Steven replied, trying to sound upbeat.

"I'm good, thank you. Sir, are you alright?" Sarah hesitated, her eyes searching his face.

Steven forced a smile.

"Yes, I'm fine. Why do you ask?"

"You seem... different. Don't let this new position overwhelm you. I'm here for you, as always. And it's not my place, but..." Sarah trailed off, concern evident in her voice.

"Thank you, Sarah. I appreciate your concern," Steven interrupted, touched by her kindness.

"If you ever need to talk, I'm here, sir," Sarah offered.

"Thanks; that means a lot," Steven said, genuinely grateful. It felt good to have someone care about his well-being. "Hold my calls, please. I have an unexpected meeting upstairs. I'll be back soon," he added.

“Of course, see you later,” Sarah replied, her concern evident as Steven headed upstairs.

Steven climbed the stairs, thinking about the unexpected meeting. Out of all the possibilities, he didn’t need more complications, especially if they involved Drake.

“Steven, Mr. Weber is waiting for you,” Weber’s secretary informed him as he approached the executive office.

“Thank you,” Steven replied, taking a deep breath before entering.

“Ah, Steven, good morning!” his boss roared. “I appreciate your dedication. Promoting you was the right choice.”

“Thank you, Mr. Weber. What’s this about, if I may ask?” Steven asked, curious but wary.

“You don’t play about, do you? Let me get straight to it. We’re not just partnering with CSoft; they’ll be a subsidiary of Jada. We need someone to oversee their plant's transition to our standards,” Mr. Weber explained, his eyes gleaming with anticipation. “You’ll be staying at the Regency Hotel's presidential suite in Mexico for a month. Feel free to bring Lisa along if you’d like.”

Steven hesitated, thinking of his strained relationship with Lisa.

“Thank you, Weber, but I don’t think she’ll be joining me.”

"If that changes, let me know. The company jet will be ready. Can you leave for CSoft this evening?" Mr. Weber asked.

"This evening? I—" Steven repeated, taken aback.

"Yes, is that a problem?" Mr. Weber interrupted.

"Uh, no, it's... it's fine. I'll meet with the IT team and pack my things. I'll be ready in a few hours."

"Excellent; I knew we could count on you. With the stock situation and last quarter's results, I didn't want to go myself. A reporter will be visiting later," Mr. Weber added.

"I'll keep you updated," Steven assured him.

"And keep me posted on your progress. Maybe we can play golf when I visit. You do play, right?"

"I do, but it's been a while," Steven admitted. "I might be a little rusty since I've been focused on the new job."

"Don't forget, golf is as important as office work at your level. Most meetings will be on the course now," Mr. Weber advised.

"I understand; I'll remember that," Steven said, trying to hide his reservations. "I'll keep you informed."

As Steven left the office, he was brimming with varying thoughts. He was grateful for the promotion and couldn't believe he had gotten it. It didn't make him as happy as he thought, but his stomach turned at the prospect of Drake Foster getting the promotion instead of him.

On the plus side, maybe this new role would mean less travel, as he hoped. Traveling had lost its charm over time for him. Then he reflected on his marriage, in which they had been mostly apart due to his frequent travels. In fact, there had been one difficult year when he spent almost ten months solely traveling for work.

"Sarah, could you please call Mr. Patty from IT and ask him to come up?" Steven requested, his mind still processing the sudden trip to Mexico.

"Of course, sir. Did your meeting go well?" Sarah inquired, her tone filled with curiosity.

"Yes, it did. Unexpectedly, I have to head to Mexico. I'll arrange for you to join me in a few days if that's alright with you," Steven replied.

"Really? That sounds wonderful! I could use the vacation. I'll let you know when Mr. Patty arrives," Sarah said, sounding pleased at the prospect of a break.

Steven chuckled at the thought of bringing his secretary along with him instead of his wife, who was more excited than Lisa ever could be. A month was a long time, yet he didn't even think to immediately let Lisa know he had to go away for a whole month, thinking she wouldn't care.

He wasn't surprised that Lisa had built a life without him. When a marriage was held together by nothing more than a legal document, it was easier to walk away than to try to mend it, even if it meant changing oneself. The only connection between them was a piece of paper from the state of California. But now, Steven was determined to level the playing field.

Steven sifted through emails as he waited, his thoughts drifting to Mr. Patty, a retired military officer. He trusted him without a doubt; Mr. Patty was known for his dedication and preferred working alone. Despite his private nature, he felt a sense of duty to help other Black men achieve their goals.

Aside from that, Steven always found Mr. Patty's stories from his time in the army fascinating. A career soldier, he saw the military as his ticket out of the challenging environment he grew up in. Basic training had been a shock for him.

"I never interacted with a white man until I arrived at Fort Jackson," Mr. Patty would say, referring to it as "the hole."

***

Mr. Patty often spoke fondly of his time in the army, where everyone, regardless of background, was treated equally. Everyone faced the same challenges and rigorous training. The experience was level, pushing each individual to stand out by going above and beyond. Growing up in Chicago's inner city, Mr. Patty had never ventured far from home before heading south for basic training. He vividly remembered the sweltering heat of the long bus ride, which seemed impossible at the time.

During basic training, Mr. Patty was paired with Private Boyd, a white recruit from Washington State. Despite their differences, they had never interacted closely with someone of the other's race.

Boyd came from a privileged background, and Mr. Patty often wondered why he had chosen the military at all. But in the army, personal backgrounds didn't matter; completing the mission did. The training forced them to work together, each responsible for the other's success or failure.

It wasn't until a grueling field exercise that Mr. Patty began to see Boyd in a new light. Boyd confided in him about his troubled family life. His father was abusive, taking out his anger on Boyd. To protect his younger sister, Boyd endured the abuse silently. His mother was too afraid to intervene, often trying to appease her husband at any cost.

As Mr. Patty listened, Boyd shared a harrowing story from when his mother was hospitalized for coccydynia, a painful condition. Boyd's father had tried to explain it away as a "woman's problem," but when police were called due to suspicions of rape, Boyd's mother was too frightened to confirm it.

Through these conversations, Mr. Patty came to understand the depth of Boyd's emotional scars. His mother felt trapped, with nowhere else to go, accepting their situation as nothing less than hell. Boyd's growing concern for his mother led him to research her medical condition. What he discovered horrified him. Seeing his mother, the woman who had raised him, live in such pain was unbearable.

He urged her to leave his abusive father, but she remained adamant in her decision to stay. Frustrated and desperate for change, Boyd made the painful choice to leave home, and the military offered him an escape and a chance for a better life.

The breaking point came when Boyd noticed a change in his younger sister's behavior. After a business trip with their father to Sacramento, she became withdrawn, spending hours locked in her room, crying her eyes out. Boyd suspected the worst—that his father had been molesting her. Confronting his father then led to a violent altercation, but Boyd stood his ground. His father's chilling words, "The day you graduate, you better not come home, or you will leave here... dead," rebounded in Boyd's mind long after he left.

After completing basic training, Mr. Patty and Boyd lost touch despite their promise to stay connected. Mr. Patty often wondered about Boyd's fate, hoping he had found peace and safety.

"In many ways, the military was a blessing for Boyd," Mr. Patty would tell Steven, "but it also took a lot from him. The military reshapes you entirely, stripping away your old self and rebuilding you from scratch."

Steven always intently empathized with Boyd's struggles.

"The story that resonates with me," Steven shared, "is how the military took so much from Boyd. I can't claim to fully understand the life of a soldier, but I can relate to the sacrifices made. Serving in the military means you pay a price, only to return to find a changed home and strangers in place of loved ones."

After returning from his second tour in what he called "the desert," Mr. Patty's life also tore apart at the seams. His wife left him for a younger soldier, and his relationship with his children became strained.

His enthusiasm for military life waned, especially after being denied a promotion to E-9. Feeling lost, Mr. Patty transitioned into a telecommunications and security job at Jada. Though the pay was better, it wasn't substantial.

Still, it provided him with the flexibility to seek help for his lingering mental health issues from the VA (Veteran Affairs).

***

"Mr. Blackman, Mr. Patty is here. Should I send him in?" Sarah's voice came over the intercom.

"Yes, please send him in. Hold my calls after this meeting," Steven instructed.

Mr. Patty then entered, his demeanor direct and no-nonsense. His military discipline was apparent in everything he did, and his attire was immaculate.

"Have a seat, Mr. Patty. How have you been?" Steven asked politely.

"I'm well, thank you. Congrats on the promotion! Keep setting the example," Mr. Patty responded.

"Ah, thanks a ton. How's IT treating you?" Steven asked, genuinely interested.

"I mostly keep to myself and get the job done. People think I'm rude, but as long as the work's done, I can't say I care."

Steven nodded and then tried to steer the conversation toward a potential leadership role in IT. "Listen, I've heard there's a leadership position coming up in IT."

"I'm not interested," Mr. Patty cut in. "I like keeping things simple."

Steven sensed there was more to Mr. Patty's discretion.

"I appreciate your perspective. Do you do any work outside of Jada?"

"I stay updated on industry advancements to help Jada prepare for the future," Mr. Patty replied.

Steven hesitated to talk to Mr. Patty about a particularly sensitive subject, which was more personal than professional.

"I have a personal issue that I need your help on. I need someone I can trust. Can I be upfront with you... to the point?"

"Anything we discuss is between us. That's how I do things," Mr. Patty urged.

Clearing his throat, Steven finally spoke. "I…I suspect my wife is cheating on me. I don't have proof, but I've noticed her closeness with another friend of ours, and it's... unsettling. My gut doesn't often lie to me."

Mr. Patty's military-trained composure dithered for a moment, not from shock at Steven's revelation but from the trust placed in him. A flicker of disbelief crossed his face.

"Mr. Blackman, you've always had your life together. How could this happen?"

"Beats me."

"I understand your frustration, but I'm not equipped to investigate," Mr. Patty admitted.

"You are, Mr. Patty. And you'd also be looking for answers if you were in my shoes. I don't want to do this anymore because, frankly, I'm exhausted. Everything is becoming a little too much to handle, and this promotion, as new and shiny as it is, doesn't much help."

Mr. Patty paused for a moment.

"What exactly do you want me to do?"

Steven walked up to him and said gravely, "I need discreet cameras installed at my house and a tracker on my wife's car. I want to be sure about this."

"Installing cameras is something you could do yourself with the right equipment. But I'll help you find the best options," Mr. Patty offered.

"I need your expertise to make sure she doesn't suspect anything. I want to be certain," Steven insisted.

Contemplating for a moment, Mr. Patty said, “Let’s plan to meet this weekend to discuss it further.”

Shaking his head, Steven replied, “I’ll be in Mexico for weeks. You’ll need to handle everything. Money’s no object; I just need to trust you,” Steven said.

“It’s not that simple, Mr. Blackman...” Mr. Patty hesitated.

Steven then went over to his desk and pulled out a large envelope from his drawer. He handed it to Mr. Patty.

"Inside, you’ll find everything you need: house alarm codes, her car’s VIN, her schedule. I want you to monitor her shop too,” Steven explained.

Smacking his lips, Mr. Patty tried to gauge Steven’s intent: "This is a serious request. Are you sure about this?”

“Yes. You’re the only one I trust with this. Not even Peter knows,” Steven replied.

Mr. Patty took a moment to consider, then returned the items to the envelope. He took a deep breath and made up his mind.

“You’ve always treated me with respect, never acting like you were above me,” Mr. Patty sighed. “You listen when I speak. Okay, I’ll help you.”

Relieved, Steven patted Mr. Patty on the back and said, “Good, man. I’ll be away for about a month. I hope we’ll have everything sorted by then.”

"I'll do my best. I'll need to assess the areas at your home and her shop to install the equipment," Mr. Patty responded. "And I'll need to upgrade my system for this and set up a discreet internet access point at your home."

"Fine by me. I want full surveillance: her comings and goings, who she meets, and everything about them. Don't overlook anything," Steven emphasized.

"No one will suspect a thing," Mr. Patty assured him.

"We can't talk about this until you have a full report. No calls. And let's keep this between us," Steven cautioned.

Steven handed over an envelope filled with wads of cash. "This should cover it. If it's not enough, I'll provide more."

"It should suffice. I'll come to you if I need anything extra," Mr. Patty said.

Steven nodded when he suddenly glanced out the window and spotted Drake Foster passing by.

"That guy... is the bane of my existence. One day, he'll get what he deserves."

Mr. Patty caught a glimpse of Drake's reflection.

"I can't stand him either. Some people you just tolerate until their time comes."

"Anyway, thank you, Mr. Patty. I appreciate your help and look forward to your findings," Steven said, extending his hand.

"Thank you, Mr. Blackman. It's important to remember our roots and how we got here," Mr. Patty replied, shaking Steven's hand with a tight grip.

"Freedom's never free, is it?" Steven added gratefully.

With a silent exchange and a deal made, Mr. Patty left the room, knowing what he had to do now.

Watching Mr. Patty leave, Steven gathered his belongings to head out of the office. He felt confident about his decision, no matter how twisted it was. It was time to face the truth.

Chapter 10: The Loneliness Calls

The night before had felt like a dream. It almost didn't seem real to Lisa; she had a hard time wrapping her head around the whirlwind of a night she'd had.

But now, it was time to step out of la-la land and plant her feet back on the ground. She still felt the haze of emotions from her night with Drake, but she quickly pushed the thoughts aside. She had to focus. Steven was home, and the last thing she wanted was an uncomfortable conversation or even a silent exchange of stares that hinted at unspoken truths.

Lisa decided she'd head to the store earlier than usual today. She told herself it was to get a jump start on the inventory, but deep down, she knew it was to avoid Steven. The thought of facing him after last night brought unease. Her time with Drake had been electrifying, almost intoxicating, and now the reality of her marriage loomed before her like a heavy cloud. She figured burying herself in work would be the best way to distract herself and shake off the guilt that had started to stress her.

At the store, Lisa poured herself into the work. She went through the inventory with laser focus, reorganized shelves, and made notes for future stock orders. For a moment, she felt her control returning, compartmentalizing everything. Work had always been her refuge, a place where the chaos of her personal life couldn't reach her.

However, as the day wore on, Lisa found herself looking at the clock more often than she liked. She knew she couldn't stay at the store forever. Eventually, she had to go home.

As she pulled into the driveway, her chest tightened at the sight of Steven's car parked neatly in the garage. Parking the car, she took a deep breath as if mentally preparing herself for a possible confrontation. With her hands gripping on the steering wheel and her head resting on it, this was not the ideal start to the day, but she had to face the music sooner or later.

Lisa's footsteps dragged as she got out of the car, slamming the car door shut forcefully. She stepped into the house, greeted only by silence and the remnants of shattered memories scattered across the floor.

"Honey?" she called out to him, her eyes scanning the room as she stepped over the shards of glass, her voice echoing through the empty rooms. "What the hell? You home?"

But there was no response. Just a shroud of silence. Still, Steven's message was conveyed in the broken shards on the floor. "He's gone," she muttered to herself, a twinge of guilt troubling her conscience.

Panic crept into her tone as she searched the house. *Where are you?*

Finally reaching the bedroom, Lisa's breath stopped for a moment at the sight before her. The door stood slightly ajar, revealing the aftermath of Steven's emotional outburst. She gasped, her hands flying to her mouth in shock.

She knelt down to pick up what was left of the picture frame of their wedding, clutching the torn image to her chest. She felt a surge of regret wash over her. "Oh my God! Steven, what have you done?" she whispered.

But in the chaos, Lisa's thoughts turned to one thing—her pearls. With hurried steps, she crossed the room, the broken glass crunching beneath her heels. "The pearls..." she murmured anxiously, her heart sprinting with fear.

As she reached for the jewelry box, relief flooded through her when she found them still intact. Her fingers brushed against the smooth pearls of her necklace, untouched and serene on the velvet cloth. At that moment, she recognized the true significance of the pearls. It wasn't out of any sense of vanity or being egocentric; in fact, it was the exact opposite.

The pearls were a gift from Steven, encapsulating their love and journey thus far. They represented Steven's love, a symbol of his affection for her that once was a force to be reckoned with.

Steven's gesture spoke volumes despite their struggles, reaffirming her feelings for him. As she cradled the pearls close to her heart, a ray of hope flickered in her—one of opportunity amid the shattered pieces of their relationship.

Lisa was lost in a world that didn't appear to care about her suffering as she struggled to accept her newfound "freedom." She had longed to be free of her marriage the night before, but now that she was looking at the chaos that surrounded her, the idea felt overwhelming.

As she fastened the necklace around her neck, the cool pearls offered a fleeting comfort against her skin. In a way, it eased the pain in her wounded heart. Despite the fact that the feeling was fleeting, a menacing sadness quickly settled in. Perhaps what amplified her loneliness was not just her isolation but the silence surrounding her.

With a sigh, Lisa reached for the picture on the nightstand, feeling the weight of memories pressing against her heart. When she looked herself in the mirror, caressing the supple skin on her décolletage, she was transported back to the day she had married Steven. It was a day suffused with happiness and promise, in contrast to her current despair.

Lisa contemplated the overwhelming emotions that had long been buried within her. For as long as she could remember, she had been bound to the expectations and demands of others—a legacy inherited from her mother.

Now that Steven was gone, she wasn't sure if continuing her mother's legacy was worthwhile anymore. As she began to understand her circumstances, the feeling of haunting loss faded. She couldn't just dismiss the fact that there would be a certain charm in living a life without a partner. After all, Lisa had been devoted to just one man her entire life, from high school all the way to adulthood. But the vicious cycle would end here and now.

Over the years, Steven had given her anything and everything she could ever want. The hard pill to swallow was that it simply wasn't enough anymore. She reflected on her life, and something became clearer to her: a familiar anguish of loss gave way to all the possibilities as she started to imagine a life free from the weight of other people's expectations.

"If he wants to leave, it's his loss," she mused aloud, the words carrying finality.

In that moment, the memories of sorrowful times faded, replaced by the promise of unexplored horizons and endless possibilities. Her mind ran free with ideas that had long since been buried in her heart. Joy overtook her soul for the first time in what felt like an eternity.

Lisa's epiphany was suddenly interrupted by the ringing of the doorbell. She hastily wiped away her tears, wondering who could be visiting right now. Moving across the hall to the guest bathroom, she quickly washed away the streaks of tears from her face. She didn't want to share her intimate experience with anyone.

She opened the door to an all-too-familiar face after only hours of seeing him.

"Dra—," she started to say before getting cut off.

"Where the hell have you been?" Drake's voice diffused through her thoughts as he entered, "I've called you like 50 times."

"I—" Lisa was yet again interrupted as Drake spoke over her, his frustration bubbling to the top.

"I mean, what's the point of having a phone if you're not going to answer it?"

"Stop!" Lisa yelled; her irritation was obvious. "I'm not married to *you*, so I don't owe you any explanation. And who do you think you are, showing up to my house unannounced like this?"

Lisa's abrupt response caught Drake off guard. His apology came after a moment of silence. "You're right... I shouldn't have come here. I was just... worried."

As Drake spoke, Lisa realized the instability of the situation. She couldn't risk letting Steven find out about Drake's visit, fearing it would give him the moral high ground.

"You should never come here," Lisa asserted firmly. "This is my home, and what happened between us was nothing more than a stupid, drunken mistake."

Drake contorted his face as he tried to make sense of Lisa's words. "*Mistake?* What do you mean? Life just doesn't happen, and what happened between us was meant to be."

Upset, Lisa turned and walked further inside the house, her thoughts consumed by Steven's unexpected absence. "Did Steven put you up to this? Is this about him?"

Drake's denial was swift: "Steven? No, Lisa! I saw him at the office this morning, but we don't even talk like that."

"Well, he isn't answering his phone. And that isn't like him. He at least returns my calls at some point," Lisa reasoned. Her agitation grew as she recounted the events of her return home. "When I got here, his car was in the garage, but he's nowhere to be found. The bedroom is a mess, and…" She stopped abruptly, realizing she was revealing too much. "Never mind."

Sensing her distress, Drake pulled her close. "Look, I'll make a few calls. I'm sure he's just been busy with meetings."

But Lisa pushed him away. "I don't need your help. You've done more than enough."

Confused by her reaction, Drake hesitated before speaking again. "Lisa, are you alright? What's really going on? You know you can tell me anything."

"It's nothing that concerns you," Lisa replied curtly. "Just leave, please. I need you to just go."

She wanted to say more, but she didn't want him to stay any longer than he needed to.

As Drake turned to go, Lisa's suspicions appeared to be unfounded but impossible to shake. "Look, you're right. Maybe last night was a mistake for you. But it wasn't for me."

Lisa, fuming, shot back at Drake. “What do you mean?” she asked, stomping toward him. “Steven is *gone!* Some of his clothes are gone. You knew all along, didn’t you? You were waiting for this opportunity.”

Drake stood there, stunned. “Gone?! What do you mean, *gone?”*

“Gone as in he’s not here, Drake! And I don’t know where he could be. And you being here in my house isn’t doing me any favors.” Lisa cupped her head, pacing in circles. “Just get out of my house and don’t ever say anything to me again, ever!”

With his eyes widening, Drake tried to diffuse the tension. “Take a deep breath, Lisa, and please calm down.” He waited for a moment to ensure Lisa was listening before continuing. “Now, can you please tell me what’s going on?”

“Okay, okay,” Lisa groaned, taking a deep breath. “I came home; the house was a mess, and some of his clothes were gone. I guess the day’s finally here. He’s left me. Either that or... I don’t know...” Her words trailed off.

Drake gasped, “Let’s find out, shall we?” He whipped out his phone from the inside of his coat pocket and quickly dialed Steven’s office number, the anticipation mounting as he waited for someone to pick up.

As Drake spoke into the phone, Lisa paced nervously, thinking about different possibilities and fears. She couldn’t let go of the sinking feeling that something was terribly wrong.

The conversation ended abruptly, leaving Drake visibly shaken. “What’s wrong? Where is he?” Lisa pressed.

“He’s in Mexico,” Drake rasped.

“Mexico? Really...”

“Huh. Nobody told me anything about Steven going to Mexico, and in fact, I was supposed to be leading that effort,” Drake explained. “I have to go, but I’ll see you later,” he said as he hurried out the door.

As Drake left, he noticed a gray car parked across the street, its occupant appearing suspicious. Drake approached cautiously, his senses on high alert.

“Can I help you?” Drake called out.

The driver looked up, startled. “No, thank you. Just trying to figure out this GPS mess,” he replied, passing a curt smile.

"Ah, it happens to me all the time,” Drake replied, staring at the car. “Where are you trying to go? Maybe I can help you.”

“No thanks…I got it,” the man sheepishly replied.

Drake nodded, a sense of unease settling over him. “Well, be careful. The police around here don’t take kindly to people loitering in their cars,” he warned, his eyes narrowing slightly.

“Yeah, thanks,” the driver muttered, his demeanor tense. “I’m actually moving out right now. Appreciate the advice.”

Drake watched as the car pulled away, his suspicions evident even as it disappeared from view. With a sigh, he returned to the office, his mind buzzing with unanswered questions.

Meanwhile, Lisa remained shaken by the revelation about Steven's whereabouts. With a heavy heart, she called him, her hands clammy as she dialed his number. When it went to voicemail, she hung up and sent a text instead.

"I hope all is okay. You weren't home when I came, so I called your office, and they told me about your trip to Mexico. I wish you would have told me. I felt like a fool, not knowing where my own husband was. I'm sorry about our fight. Please call me."

As she hit send, she prayed for a response—a sign that he was okay. Lisa then tossed her phone aside, sitting on the edge of the bed, her heart heavy.

Minutes ticked by like hours, each second stretching into eternity as Lisa waited anxiously for a reply. But none came.

Unable to bear the silence any longer, Lisa dialed Steven's number. "Steven, please call," she cried as her pleas in the form of calls and messages went unanswered once more.

The passing minutes felt like endless hours, each second dragging on with agonizing slowness. With each unanswered attempt to reach him, her anxiety grew, knotting her stomach with worry. Alone in her thoughts, she couldn't shake the unease that settled over her like a heavy blanket. The silence in the house was deafening; each moment was punctuated only by the sound of her own breathing and the sounds of distant traffic.

With each passing hour, Lisa's hope waned, replaced by helplessness. She felt trapped in a cycle of waiting and uncertainty, unable to move forward until she heard from Steven. Then, it dawned on her: her freedom began to feel more like a curse.

As the night wore on, her exhaustion grew, both physically and emotionally. She longed for the comfort of sleep, yet her mind refused to rest, consumed by worry and fear. In the darkness of her room, she felt more alone than ever. Lisa, all alone, curled up in her king-sized bed and slept, wallowing in grief.

As the night passed by and the sun rose, Lisa's despair grew deeper. Her eyes fluttered open in the bright morning light, and she felt the loneliness inside her surfacing. Tears streamed down her cheeks as she looked up at the ceiling. Her voice choked as she cried out to the heavens in a last-ditch effort. "Oh Lord, I need you right now," she prayed, desperate for help. "I need you to say yes when everything around me says no," she cried, tears staining the pillow.

Chapter 11: Facing the Abyss

Steven adjusted the crisp white sleeves of his button-down shirt, a stark contrast to the sunbaked Mexican landscape outside his window. He took a long sip from the steaming mug of coffee he had grabbed on his way out the door, the rich aroma momentarily grounding him. He glanced at his phone, a familiar pang in his chest as he saw the string of unread messages from Lisa.

Pushing the phone face down on the table, he squared his shoulders. Now wasn't the time for distractions. He turned on his laptop, the bright screen illuminating the resolute set of his jaw. He scanned the emails detailing the project's progress. He scheduled a meeting with his team for the afternoon. A plan—a clear and actionable one—was beginning to take shape in his mind. It was time to dissect the situation, assess the damage, and find a way forward, both for the project and for his own life.

He jotted down key points on a notepad, his penmanship sharp and focused. As the clock ticked closer to the meeting time, Steven felt a gush of purpose course through him. He wouldn't let chaos win.

He would make it through this professionally and personally, one calculated step at a time. He straightened his tie in the reflection of his laptop screen, the image of a man ready to face whatever came his way.

While he displayed a strong demeanor, his heart ached to speak to Lisa. She had always been his rock, a safe harbor where unspoken anxieties could be calmed with a simple touch or a shared silence. Even if she couldn't always fix things, her presence made his burdens feel lighter.

He sighed, running a hand through his hair, a nervous habit he hadn't realized had returned. Looking at the clock again, he noticed there was still an hour before his meeting. It was a small window, but maybe it was enough.

With a deep breath, he dialed his sister Brandie's number. The phone was pressed cool against his ear, each ring echoing the anxious rhythm of his heart. Maybe, he thought, Brandie could offer some clarity amidst the growing chaos.

Thankfully, the wait was short.

"Steven! How are you doing? I'm so glad you called," Brandie's voice burst through the receiver, brimming with sunshine and a hint of surprise. "Believe it or not, I was just thinking about you and Lisa."

Steven forced a smile, the muscles in his face resisting the effort.

"Hey, sis," he replied. "Just called to see how you and the family are doing. By the sound of your voice, everything's going great?"

Unconsciously, he began doodling on his notepad, the pen leaving a trail of nervous scribbles.

"We are great, Steven!" Brandie's voice buzzed with excitement. "Work is crazy busy, but guess what? I got promoted! I even have my own team now. It's a lot, but...exhilarating, I guess that's the word."

Her chirpy voice painted a clear picture of her joy.

"Good for you, sis. It's about time they recognized your talent," Steven said, managing a grunt of acknowledgment.

He forced a lightness into his voice that didn't quite reach his eyes.

"Thanks! And yes, a raise came with the promotion, a nice one too, if I do say so myself."

A small smile touched Steven's lips.

"That's fantastic. Maybe I can borrow a little to get by down here in Mexico."

It was a joke, a desperate attempt at normalcy, and it landed with a dull thud.

"Wait—Mexico?" Brandie's voice rose slightly, caught off guard. "What are you doing in Mexico?"

"Yeah, had to come down here for work, you know. My job never gives me a break," Steven replied smoothly. "But enough about me. How are the boys doing? Keeping you busy, I bet."

Brandie chuckled, still not fully convinced by the reaction.

"Um, yes, the boys are doing well. They're growing like weeds! Another month, and they'll be out for summer break. You know what that means, right? Time for the annual camping trip with their favorite uncle!" she teased.

Steven's mind conjured images of laughter around crackling campfires, sticky marshmallows, and endless games of tag in the woods. It was a tradition he cherished, a chance to escape the daily grind and bond with his nephews. Being a role model for those energetic boys had always been one of the highlights of his year.

A pang of sadness shot through him as he realized the uncertainty surrounding this year's trip. Brandie's smile faltered slightly on the other end. She caught the hesitation in Steven's voice, a subtle hitch that spoke volumes.

A buried memory, a familiar ache, threatened to resurface. Growing up, their childhood had been a landscape painted in hues of absence. Their father had vanished before they were old enough to understand what had transpired. Consequently, the responsibility of holding their family together fell on their mother's strong shoulders, leaving a void that no love could entirely fill.

Brandie understood, perhaps better than anyone, the importance of these camping trips for all of them. They were more than just an escapade; they were a chance to create the positive male influence she and Steven never had. A pang of longing, a what-if, brushed through her, reminding her of the experiences they had missed in their childhood.

Then, pushing the memory aside, she forced a smile.

"They really look forward to it, you know," she said, her words aimed not just at Steven but also at the ghosts of their past. "Better enjoy these moments, Steven. They grow up fast, and before you know it, they'll be teenagers too cool to be seen with any of us uncool adults."

A hint of wistfulness colored her voice, an indirect acknowledgment of the short-lived nature of childhood and the precious bond they shared.

The silence stretched, heavier than the usual comfortable quiet that sometimes fell between them. The carefree banter they usually enjoyed seemed strained, substituted by tension cracking down the phone line. Brandie noticed how Steven hadn't spoken much during the call, and his usual easy replies seemed replaced by short bursts of agreement. Creases of concern fixed themselves onto her brow.

"Listen, it sounds like something's on your mind. You didn't call just to chat about the boys, did you, Steven? What's really going on?"

Steven hesitated, running a hand through his hair in a silence that spoke volumes to his sister. A forced smile tugged at the corners of his lips.

"Why does something have to be wrong, Brandie? Can't a guy just call his favorite sister to say hello?"

Brandie wasn't so easily fooled—they knew each other too well.

"Of course, you can," she said, her tone softening further. "But I know you, Steven. What's going on… is Lisa alright?"

Despair seemed to consume him, reflected in the slump of his shoulders.

"You got me," he admitted. "I could never fool you with anything. Brandie… I think Lisa is having an affair." A bitter taste coated his tongue as he spoke the words aloud.

Brandie fell silent as the force of his confession made its space between them. The revelation dangled like a dark cloud.

"Steven, you're just imagining things. Lisa would never do that. You guys have been married since forever," she finally said, her voice masked with a hope that seemed to falter even as she spoke it.

"Married, yes. I thought I knew her better than anyone else," Steven countered.

His suspicion had been building for days, fueled by Lisa's distant behavior.

"But lately, things haven't felt right. She's been acting strange—cold and withdrawn. She avoids me whenever possible, and…" he hesitated, his voice trailing off.

"And what, Steven?" Brandie prompted gently. She cared deeply for both her brother and Lisa, and the thought of infidelity tearing their relationship apart was a painful one. "Do you have any proof? Did you see something, or is this just a feeling?"

Steven sighed, running a hand through his hair yet again.

"No, no proof," he admitted. "It's just a gut feeling, a gnawing suspicion that won't go away. But how can I ignore it, Brandie? Every time I look at her, I wonder…" he said, unable to finish.

"Steven, listen, accusations are serious things, especially without proof. Have you tried talking to Lisa? Maybe there's a simple explanation for her behavior," Brandie said gently.

A frustrated sigh escaped Steven's lips.

"Talking? We barely have conversations anymore. It's like we're living parallel lives under the same roof. I remember those nights we used to spend talking for hours, sharing dreams and anxieties. Now, silence hangs between us, heavy and suffocating."

"Marriage takes work, Steven," Brandie reminded him. "Maybe you both got caught up in the daily grind. You with your demanding job, and Lisa…" she hesitated, searching for the right words.

"Lisa, with what?" Steven prompted.

"Well, forget it," Brandie continued cautiously, "let's be honest about you for now. You travel a lot for work. How much quality time do you actually spend together?"

Steven winced. He knew his sister was right. His career in finance had taken off in recent years, demanding long hours and frequent trips abroad. He had prided himself on being the provider, the rock for his wife, but lately, a nagging doubt had begun to creep in.

Was he neglecting the emotional requirements of their relationship?

"I know, I know," he mumbled. "But my work..."

Brandie's voice sharpened. "Is that all you think about, Steven? Always buried in work? Look, I get that you want to provide, but there's more to marriage than financial security. How can Lisa be expected to feel connected to you if you're never around and always occupied with Jada?"

Steven clenched his jaw, defiance rising within him.

"Look, all I know is work! It's where I shine. And taking care of the woman in my life is my duty! Why can't she see that?"

The last part came out defensive, a knee-jerk reaction to the guilt nibbling at him. Was his dedication to providing a comfortable life for Lisa backfiring? Was his absence creating a void she couldn't bear? Maybe, a cruel voice whispered in the back of his mind, she was filling that void with someone else.

"...And don't even get me started on kids. You two haven't even brought that up, have you?" Brandie countered, undeterred.

Steven flinched at the mention of children. It was a topic they'd circled for years, a silent understanding that felt more like a comfortable avoidance.

"It just hasn't been the right time," he mumbled, the truth a bitter pill to swallow.

The unspoken issue of children loomed large, a constant shadow cast by their career ambitions and his relentless travel schedule.

Brandie sighed.

"Steven, listen. Maybe 'the right time' won't magically appear. Life has a way of throwing curveballs, and sometimes, you just have to adjust. But the truth is, you can't keep putting things on hold forever. Marriage is a partnership, and a successful one requires presence and effort from both sides."

A heavy silence descended between them, thick with implicit truths. Steven stared out the window, the bustling city lights blurring into a kaleidoscope of emotions. Brandie's words echoed in his mind, each one a hammer blow chipping away at the carefully constructed facade he'd built.

Steven could see that his sister was not wrong in her assessment. His relentless pursuit of success had come at a cost, a cost he was only now beginning to understand. The glamorous international trips and the late nights at the office had all seemed so important at the time. But now, the emptiness of his hotel room mirrored the hollowness he felt inside.

"I don't think she hates you, Steven," Brandie said gently, sensing his growing turmoil. "She may be hurt and feel less important, but your work and Jada always come first. Come on… I'm sure you two have had these conversations in the past. This shouldn't be anything new?"

"No, we haven't spoken in the last few days," Steven admitted. "I'm in Mexico for a few weeks on a business trip."

"Mexico…?" Brandie echoed.

"Yes, Mexico," Steven confirmed, a knot of tension tightening in his gut.

He hadn't planned on confiding in Brandie about the trip, which was a selfish attempt to punish Lisa for her perceived coldness. But the truth, like a stubborn weed, had a way of pushing through the cracks.

"She knows I'm here. She's called a few times, but I didn't pick up. I'm just… angry, Brandie. Here I am, busting my butt to give her everything, and it's never enough."

There was a dark suspicion festering like a wound in his gut. Maybe Lisa’s calls weren't about him at all. Maybe she was scrambling to cover up some mistake, some secret she didn't want him to find out about.

The image of Lisa, laughing and carefree with another man, was a mental blow that left Steven reeling. It was a picture his mind couldn't seem to shake, a vivid nightmare playing on repeat.

"Steven, listen, there may be some truth to that, but you have to see things from her perspective. If I were in her shoes, with you gone for weeks, barely a phone call, I'd be pretty darn mad, too. You haven't exactly been Mr. Attentive Husband lately."

Steven bristled, his jaw gritting.

"Mad?! So, you're telling me if I was never around, you'd just... find someone else?" The idea of his own sister seemingly defending Lisa's actions was infuriating.

"Steven, honey, calm down. There's a difference between being mad and having an affair. Look, I love you; you're my brother, but sometimes you can be so thickheaded. Snap out of it and call your wife. Talk to her and see what's going on. Jumping to conclusions without any proof isn't going to solve anything."

Steven listened with a crumpled brow, but his mind was a tangled mess. Brandie's words bounced around his skull like pebbles, none of them finding purchase. He was lost in a labyrinth of his own making, fueled by suspicion and betrayal.

Was Lisa truly unhappy? Had his persistent pursuit of success driven a wedge between them, leaving her feeling lonely and neglected? And the darkest question of all: was she seeing someone else because of being deserted?

The thought sent anger crashing through him, a feeling threatening to consume him whole. He clasped his fists, his knuckles turning white.

He needed answers, and he needed them *now*.

The room felt like it was closing in on him, the silence pressing down on his already frayed nerves. *Should he call Lisa?*

"Steven, do you hear me?" Brandie's voice cut through his internal battle. The concern in her tone was unmistakable. "If you want to save your marriage, call her. Do you?"

Steven stared out the window, lost in his thoughts.

"Yes… maybe," he mumbled.

He did love Lisa, and of that, there was no doubt. But the hurt and suspicion bothered him, making it difficult to see clearly.

"Then call her! Otherwise, don't blame anyone but yourself for whatever happens," Brandie's voice sharpened with impatience.

The force in her voice startled him. Brandie wasn't known for losing her cool, and her words struck a chord deep within him.

Could a single phone call bridge the emotional chasm between them? The answer was uncertain, but the silence on the other end of the line with Brandie was an earsplitting answer in itself.

"Alright, I will call her first thing tomorrow," Steven conceded, a defeated sigh escaping his lips.

"Tomorrow? Why not now?"

Steven rubbed a hand over his tired eyes.

"I have meetings scheduled for the rest of the day. By the time I'm free, it will probably be late at night, and Lisa will likely be asleep or busy." The excuses tasted like ash in his mouth, even to him.

"Oh, Steven. This is exactly what I'm talking about! Women want to know their man would move mountains to reach them. Call her now!"

"Are you sure?" he mumbled, the question barely audible.

The silence on the other end of the line was a blunt answer. Brandie had hung up.

Steven stared at his phone, the metal cool against his ear. His chest ached with a cocktail of emotions ranging from guilt, anger, and a growing fear. He'd been battling with his suspicions for days, the accusations churning in his gut like a bad meal. Brandie's words boomed in his mind, a harsh but undeniable truth.

He had no proof, no concrete evidence to support his growing paranoia.

Yet, the image of Lisa laughing with someone else replayed on a loop in his head, a cruel mental torture. It was a scene fueled by a lack of communication, a distance that had grown wider with every passing mile he'd traveled for work. He was at a crossroads, a desolate intersection where guilt and rage collided.

On one hand, a wave of shame seemed to consume him. He knew he hadn't exactly been the picture-perfect husband. He'd been so focused on building their future that he'd neglected the foundation: their relationship.

But the other side of the coin glinted with a cold fury. The mere suggestion of Lisa betraying him and breaking their vows made him furious all over again. And saying sorry for something she did? *No way.*

Still, a sliver of doubt remained. *Was his anger a defense mechanism, a shield against a deeper truth he wasn't ready to face?*

Steven sank into the plush armchair. He knew he needed to decide: would he confront Lisa with his suspicions, fueled by a brew of emotions and a lack of evidence? Or would he swallow his pride, pick up the phone, and try to bridge the emotional abyss he had helped create?

Maybe they could fix things, even though he knew he played a part in the mess. Steven wasn't sure what to say. An apology felt hollow, but staying silent didn't feel right either. He took a deep breath, trying to calm his racing heart.

Picking up his phone, he found Lisa's number and pressed the call. Each ring echoed in the tense silence of the room. It went on and on until, finally, it went to voicemail.

Steven stared at the phone, his finger hovering over the record button. He wanted to say something, anything, but the words wouldn't come. Leaving a message felt pointless without knowing if she'd even listen.

Maybe it's best to wait and see if she calls back, Steven thought to himself.

He hung up with a sigh. The future, it seemed, was on hold.

Chapter 12: Shifting Loyalties

The insistent buzzing of the alarm clock clawed Steven from sleep. He swatted at it blindly, the irritating sound finally silenced. Sunlight, pale and tentativc at this early hour, slanted through the window.

For a blissful moment, Steven lay still, the remnants of a dream clinging to him like cobwebs. It was a dream of laughter and sunshine, a domestic scene painted in warm hues. A jolt ran through him as reality intruded. He wasn't at home, curled up next to Lisa. He was in Mexico, thousands of miles away, and their comfortable routine was a distant memory.

The previous days' turmoil surfaced a bitter cocktail of anger, guilt, and a gnawing fear. He pushed himself out of bed, the crisp sheets a stark contrast to the confusion within him. He showered under the hot water, a temporary shield against the emotional chill. As he brushed his teeth, the acrid taste of toothpaste mingled with the metallic tang of regret.

"Work," he muttered, the word a mantra.

Work would be his refuge, a structured world where anxieties wouldn't cloud his judgment. He threw on a suit, the fabric offering a sense of control, even if it was an illusion. Downstairs, the hotel coffee tasted like burnt cardboard, but he forced it down, the caffeine a jolt to his sluggish system.

He sat down at the breakfast buffet, the clatter of plates and murmur of conversation a dull backdrop to his racing thoughts. Every instinct screamed at him to call Lisa, to hear her voice, to bridge the chasm that had grown between them. But the memory of their last strained conversation held him back. What would he even say? Accusations without proof felt hollow, a desperate attempt to regain control of a situation that was rapidly spiraling out of his grasp.

Heaving a sigh, he pulled out his laptop, the glow of the screen transitorily banishing the shadows that lurked at the corners of his vision. He scanned his emails, and each message was a task, a deadline, or a small victory he could achieve. For all its frustrations, work offered the clarity his personal life lacked.

But even as he dived into project reports and budget spreadsheets, Lisa's face kept flashing through his mind. The memory of her smile, the warmth of her touch, blatantly juxtaposed with the hollowness in his chest. He shut his eyes briefly, the image of their life together a bittersweet ache.

Pushing his laptop aside, Steven reached for his phone. He stared at the screen, Lisa's name a silent accusation. Was a simple call enough? Could it mend the broken trust and bridge the emotional distance?

He didn't have the answers but knew the silence wasn't working.

Chewing on a cold piece of toast, Steven stared out the window. The vibrant morning light in Mexico, usually a source of fascination, seemed muted today. His marriage, once a solid structure built on love and shared dreams, now felt like a house of cards teetering on the edge of collapse. Cracks had been appearing for a while, whispers of discontent growing louder with each passing day.

Had he, in his inexorable chase of success, become blind to Lisa's silent pleas for connection? The conversation with Brendie echoed in his mind, a harsh but indisputable truth. Years of missed dinners and work trips that stretched into weeks, all in the name of building a comfortable life together, a life that now felt empty and devoid of warmth. He'd seen the gradual shift in Lisa, the sparkle in her eyes fading, replaced by a cold distance that mirrored the growing chasm between them.

How could I have expected a different outcome? Steven thought to himself as the guilt gnawed at him.

Lisa deserved better. Yet, the thought of her infidelity felt like a betrayal that defied logic. Everything he'd done, all the long hours, the relentless travel, it was all to provide for her, to secure their future.

Lost in a maze of conflicting emotions, he barely registered the arrival of his remaining breakfast. Scrambled eggs sat congealing on his plate, the toast stiff and dry. Suddenly, a voice cut through his reverie.

"Good morning, sir," a young bellhop chirped, his smile bright and eager to please. "Your car is ready."

Steven looked up, startled out of his thoughts. "Thank you," he mumbled, the words tasting like ash in his mouth. "I'll be down in a minute."

Around the hotel, whispers swirled about the CEO, Ms. Rodriguez. *A force to be reckoned with*, they called her. This was just the distraction Steven needed, a chance to focus on something other than the chaos within him.

He had a meeting with Ms. Rodriguez scheduled for the morning, and for the first time since waking up, a splinter of anticipation pierced through the fog of worry.

He pushed his plate away, the uneaten breakfast—a reflection of his churning stomach. Work, a new challenge, a chance to prove himself, was a salvation he desperately needed right now. He would throw himself into the meeting, hoping the day would pass in a blur, each passing minute taking him one step further away from the wreckage of his personal life, at least for now.

But the comfort of work came with a price.

Due to security concerns, Jada, the head of corporate security at his company, had kept a tight leash on Steven's movements while in Mexico. Rigid schedules and pre-approved itineraries were a compromise he'd had to make, a stark dissimilarity to the freedom he normally enjoyed on business trips.

Still, the prospect of the Rodriguez meeting held a strange allure, a promise of distraction from his anxieties. He arrived at the sleek, modern office building a little before nine, the polished chrome and glass reflecting the morning sun.

It was an early day for Steven's secretary, Sarah. She waited patiently, a steaming cup of coffee in hand.

"Good morning, sir. Would you like some coffee before the meeting? I wasn't sure what refreshments they might have, but I requested coffee, orange juice, and bagels," she greeted him with a tight smile.

"Yes, coffee would be great," Steven mumbled, his mind still preoccupied. "And Sarah, could you please rent a car for us today? I'd like to do some sightseeing while we're here."

Sarah's eyebrows shot up in surprise. "Certainly, sir. Should I get it under your name?"

"No," Steven said, a hint of a sly smile playing on his lips. "Put it under your name, and nothing too flashy. We don't want to draw attention." He lowered his voice conspiratorially. "There's always a chance things might get a little complicated here."

Blending in, appearing less important than he was, was a strategy Steven often employed. It allowed him to assess situations and people before revealing his full capabilities. But right now, the charade served another purpose: *a temporary escape from the disorder that threatened to consume him.*

He needed this meeting, this focus on something external, anything to quiet the storm brewing inside.

"Okay," Sarah replied.

Steven, attuned to the subtle shifts in people's tone, picked up on it instantly.

"Something on your mind?" he asked with unexpected compassion.

Sarah hesitated again, then met his gaze.

"Honestly, I just wanted to thank you again for bringing me on this trip. It's a welcome change of pace, a break from the usual routine back at headquarters."

A flicker of gratitude shone in her eyes. Steven understood. With the chaos engulfing his personal life, a change of scenery was exactly what he needed, too.

Before his own thoughts could spiral back into a destructive loop, Sarah continued, holding out a folder. "Oh, and these are your messages."

Steven forced a smile, a touch of warmth replacing the earlier tension.

"Thank you, Sarah. It's a comfort to have a familiar face around, especially in a new city." He paused, then added, "By the way, when Ms. Rodriguez arrives, could you please show her straight into my office?"

"Of course, sir," she replied, a bright smile gracing her lips.

"Thanks," Steven said sincerely, taking the folder.

He realized with a jolt that he hadn't even glanced at his notes or outline for the meeting earlier that morning. His personal struggles had pushed everything else aside. Taking a deep breath, he settled into a chair, forcing himself to focus on the task at hand. He skimmed through the schedule, his brow creasing as he absorbed the details.

This meeting with Ms. Rodriguez was more complex than he initially anticipated. Perhaps that was a good thing. A complex problem demanded a complete focus, a distraction powerful enough to drown out the noise in his head.

Absorbed in the complexities of the meeting agenda, Steven scribbled notes on a legal pad. He was starting to feel a hint of control, a sense of purpose returning as he strategized his approach.

A soft knock at the door startled him from his concentration. He looked up, expecting Sarah to return with the rental car details.

Instead, the door creaked open a few inches, revealing Sarah's face. "Sir, Ms. Rodriguez is here to see you," she announced.

Steven straightened in his chair as a trace of surprise crossed his features. He'd been expecting a seasoned executive, someone hardened by years of exploring the cutthroat world of international business. Instead, Ms. Rodriguez ushered in a vision of unexpected elegance. She appeared to be in her early forties, her age betrayed only by the subtle lines carved around her eyes. Her dark hair was pulled back in a sleek chignon, highlighting the sharp angles of her jawline and the intelligent glint in her dark brown eyes. She moved with quiet confidence, her tailored black suit outlining a surprisingly athletic frame.

This wasn't the CEO Steven had envisioned, and a jolt of unexpected curiosity sparked within him.

He rose to his feet, pushing aside the unwelcome memory of Lisa, triggered perhaps by the faint, floral scent that trailed Ms. Rodriguez.

"Please, come in. Have a seat," he said, gesturing towards the conference table.

Steven forced a smile, the act momentarily pushing aside the anxieties troubling him. He turned towards Sarah, "Thank you, Sarah. Would you please close the door on your way out?"

Sarah gave a small nod, her eyes remaining for a moment on the CEO with a touch of fascination. There was an undeniable aura about Ms. Rodriguez, a quiet power that demanded attention.

"Do you need me to take notes for this meeting?" she offered.

"No, thank you, Sarah," Steven replied, his stare already returning to Ms. Rodriguez. He needed a clear head, a chance to focus on something other than the debris of his marriage.

"Good morning, Ms. Rodriguez," he continued, extending a hand in greeting. "It's a pleasure to meet you."

The corners of Ms. Rodriguez's lips curved into a smile, transforming her sharp features into something unexpectedly warm.

"Is it alright for me to call you Steven?" she asked, extending her hand.

"Absolutely, Steven will be fine. It is Ms. Rodriguez, isn't it?" his voice betrayed the emotional uproar he was trying to suppress.

Steven reached out and took her hand. He felt a pang of guilt, a prickle of awareness that this unexpected physical contact was a betrayal of Lisa, however distant she might feel right now. He forced a smile, letting go of her hand a little too abruptly. The change in his demeanor was subtle, but Ms. Rodriguez's keen eyes caught it. A glimmer of something illegible crossed her face, a momentary shadow before she composed herself and slumped into her seat. An imperceptible tension settled in the air now, a silent question mark replacing the initial ease of the encounter.

Steven felt a prickle of self-consciousness, unsure if his overly firm handshake or his abrupt withdrawal had caused the shift. He watched Ms. Rodriguez compose herself as she settled into the seat across from him.

"Ms. Rodriguez, it is. Actually, my husband passed away years ago. It's not often men in your position actively seek my input, I must say. Quite refreshing, honestly."

Steven blinked, momentarily caught off guard by her unexpected candor.

"Oh, I, uh... I'm sorry to hear that," he offered, the words sounding hollow even to his own ears.

The truth was, the news did little to dispel the unease that had settled in his gut.

A hint of amusement flashed in Ms. Rodriguez's eyes, her lips curving into a faint, enigmatic smile.

"As I said, that was a long time ago," she replied, leaning back in her chair. "Steven, you're not quite what I envisioned for this role."

Her words were delivered in a playful tone, infused with a hint of something that sent a shiver down his spine; *was it amusement or something more?*

Steven frowned, a bulge of confusion tightening in his stomach. "I don't quite understand what you mean. What were you expecting?"

"You're younger, and I dare say more handsome than the file photo did you justice. Most men in your position…well, let's just say the stress of the job tends to show," she continued with a glint in her eyes.

A warmth bloomed in Steven's cheeks, equal parts of surprise and something he couldn't quite define. There was a captivating quality to her voice, a melody accented with a hint of something exotic that drew him in.

"Thank you, ma'am," he mumbled, the formality of the address sounding awkward in the charged atmosphere.

"Now that introductions are out of the way," she said, trailing off, "please, call me Sophia. After all, we'll be working together for a fairly long time. I'd like to foster a friendly working relationship, wouldn't you?"

Steven cleared his throat, caught between the informality of her request and the undeniable pull he felt.

"Alright, ma'am—I mean, Sophia," he stammered, "Apologies, I'm not accustomed to addressing my superiors by their first name."

Sophia's smile widened, her amusement evident.

"Oh, Steven, we're not so formal down here. Relax, would you?" she chuckled.

There was an undeniable spark between them, a silent current crackling in the atmosphere. Steven felt the impulse to mirror her smile, to offer some reassurance that he was on the same page. However, the image of Lisa, a constant thorn in his side, sparkled at the back of his mind, a heavy weight that kept him fastened to his troubled reality.

"So, shall we get started with the meeting?" he finally managed to utter, breaking the charged silence that had descended upon them.

Sophia arched an eyebrow, a slight frown wrinkling her perfect forehead.

"Well, what's the hurry?" she asked, "Tell me, Steven, have you ever been to this beautiful country before, or is this your first time experiencing the magic of Mexico?"

The unexpected question caught Steven off guard.

"I've been here before," he said slowly, deciphering the sudden shift in the conversation.

By this point, a flake of understanding had begun to pierce the fog of his confusion.

Sophia's gaze held his, her smile now streaked with a hint of flirtatiousness. "I hope it's not always been for business," she continued in a husky whisper.

A pang of guilt lanced through Steven's chest, sharp and unexpected. His mind flashed back to sun-drenched beaches and whispered promises under a starlit sky, memories of a time when he and Lisa were still young and carefree. The memories came back in a flood, bittersweet and brimmed with regret.

"Not always for business, no," he replied softly.

He could almost feel the warmth of the Mexican sun on his skin and smell the sweet scent of plumeria flowers.

A subtle shift in Sophia's posture didn't escape his notice. She was leaning forward now, her earlier confident air replaced by a keen interest. It wasn't just her posture that had changed; there was a hunger in her eyes, a desire to learn more about the man sitting across from her.

"I assume you're married, then?" she inquired in a sultry purr tone as a playful pout formed on her lips.

Steven hesitated, searching for a single word that could encapsulate the tumultuous state of his marriage with Lisa.

"It's... well, let's just say it's not exactly a walk on the beach in Cancun," he finally admitted.

Sophia's eyes widened slightly, then relaxed with a hint of understanding. She averted her eyes temporarily.

"I see… well, Steven," she continued, stressing each word carefully, "whichever path your marriage takes, I sincerely wish you all the best."

Steven felt a blow course through him. The blurted-out truth now settled between them, showcasing his personal life's twisted mess. He shifted uncomfortably in his chair, the carefully constructed facade he'd maintained throughout the day threatening to crumble.

"It's more complicated than that," he finally managed to say.

He couldn't bring himself to elaborate, the details of his marriage too raw, too painful to share with a woman he barely knew.

Sophia seemed to sense his reluctance. "Absolutely," she said kindly. "Perhaps this conversation is best left for another time, a time when you're ready." She gestured towards the papers spread out on the table. "In the meantime, shall we get started on the agenda, Steven? Focusing on the project at hand might be a welcome distraction from whatever else is on your mind."

Steven nodded mutely, a wave of relief washing over him. He wasn't sure how much more he could handle veiled sympathy and the raw honesty he'd stumbled into. He forced his attention to the documents.

As they dived into the intricacies of the project, a comfortable silence descended upon them. Steven found himself impressed by Sophia's sharp intellect and her ability to grasp complex ideas with ease. He focused on the shared task, pushing aside the personal uproar that threatened to resurface.

However, a disquieting current remained. Sophia's unexpected offer of sympathy, coupled with the undeniable attraction he felt towards her, had thrown him off balance. Steven couldn't help but notice the way her voice became softer when she spoke of him, a drop of something more than just business in her gaze. He was drawn to her confident and playful nature, and for the first time in a long time, being around a woman felt easy and effortless for him.

Suddenly, Sophia broke the silence, clearing her throat, "Well, Steven, I was just thinking that Mexico is a fascinating country. Rich history, stunning scenery, delicious food... you name it. If you ever have some free time, I'd be happy to show you around. It would be a shame to miss all this place has to offer."

Steven felt a shock progress through him. He was surprised by her forwardness. Part of him, the part yearning for connection, was undeniably drawn to her confident and spirited nature. The troubles of his marriage with Lisa, along with the constant tension and rumbling bitterness, seemed to melt away in her presence.

"That sounds amazing, Sophia," he admitted.

The prospect of exploring Mexico with this captivating woman sent a thrill through him. But then, reality intruded, sharp and unwelcome.

"I'm incredibly flattered, truly," he continued, forcing a smile that felt strained even to him. "But I don't know if that would be the best idea. You know, with work and all, and upper management back home..." He trailed off, searching for an excuse that wouldn't sound entirely lame.

A playful crease formed between Sophia's brows.

"Don't worry, Steven, I wasn't suggesting anything out of line. Think of it as a professional courtesy—a local showing a business colleague the best of Mexico."

She leaned back in her chair. "After all, this country boasts a rich history and breathtaking sights, so don't forget the food! And let's just say I'm pretty good at navigating its hidden gems."

Her smile was captivating, a dazzling display of white teeth and glistening eyes. It made it incredibly difficult for Steven to refuse the appealing offer. He found himself caught between the allure of a carefree adventure with Sophia and the nagging voice of reason reminding him of the boundaries he needed to maintain.

A hesitant smile tugged at the corners of Steven's lips.

"Well, in that case, I wouldn't mind seeing some of those hidden gems you mentioned. It would be a shame to miss out," he finally conceded.

Sophia's smile widened.

"Excellent!" she exclaimed with enthusiasm. "Saturday works perfectly. How about I pick you up around…um eleven? We can make a day of it!"

Steven nodded as a lump of nervous excitement twisted in his throat.

"Saturday at eleven sounds great," Steven agreed.

The idea of exploring Mexico with Sophia was undeniably exciting, but it was also nerve-wracking. He needed to focus on the task at hand.

"Now, with that settled," he continued, clearing his throat, "let's get back to business, shall we? You were reviewing the agenda?"

"Absolutely, Steven. However, as far as I have surveyed, everything is in order based on your initial outline. You seem to have a good grasp on the project," she said.

Steven felt pride warm his chest. He'd poured a lot of work into this proposal, and Sophia's acknowledgment was a welcome validation.

"Thank you, Sophia," he replied, a genuine smile gracing his lips.

The next two hours flew by in a gush of figures, strategies, and potential roadblocks. Sophia proved to be a sharp analyst; her questions were insightful, and her suggestions were on point.

However, as they researched deeper into the details, Steven became increasingly aware of the undeniable lure bubbling between them. Sophia's gaze lingered a touch too long, her laughter too pleasant-sounding.

However, despite the growing tension, the meeting remained productive. By the time they reached the final page of the proposal, a sense of accomplishment settled over them.

"This proposal looks fantastic, Steven. You've clearly put a lot of thought and effort into it. I believe we have a very solid foundation with which to move forward.

She extended her hand towards Steven. "Now, I'm looking forward to showing you the city on Saturday, a chance to unwind after all this hard work."

Steven took her hand. He forced a smile, perhaps a little too eager, and stammered, "Absolutely, ma'am. It sounds amazing. I, uh… I can't wait. It should be a lot of fun."

He felt a trace of guilt prickle at his conscience.

Sophia's smile faltered slightly, "Call me Sophia," she said. "Wouldn't want any misunderstandings on our little Saturday outing, would we?"

Steven felt a wave of heat flood his cheeks, his blunder hitting him like a ton of bricks.

"Of course, Sophia," he mumbled.

Shame burned in his gut, the intensity of his slip-up settling heavily on him.

Sophia smiled as she reached across the table, her fingers brushing against his as she retrieved a pen.

"Don't worry about it. Just be ready for a fun-filled adventure."

As Sophia gathered her things and prepared to leave, Steven couldn't help but steal a glance at her. Her large brown eyes seemed to shimmer with desire, her smile both warm and inviting.

By the time Sophia left the office, Steven was eager to escape the lasting scent of her perfume and the memory of her touch and began packing up his belongings. His heart pounded with expectancy and guilt as he checked his voicemail.

Two messages. One had to be Lisa. He held his breath as he pressed the button to listen.

"Steven, it's Peter. Call me back when you get a chance. There's something we need to talk about... just give me a call or drop a message— I'll call you myself."

Disappointment took over Steven. Of course. It was just Peter. He deleted the message with a moan, a pang of loneliness twisting in his gut. He longed for a message from Lisa, a sign that things could be salvaged, but there was nothing.

He stared at his phone for a moment longer, the silence deafening. A muffled ache settled in his chest, conflicting with the warmth he'd felt just moments ago with Sophia.

With a sigh, he pressed the voicemail button again.

The voicemail system responded in its usual monotone. "Press seven to delete this message, or press nine to save the message." Steven, his mind preoccupied with thoughts of Lisa, absentmindedly pressed seven. "Your message has been deleted," the system confirmed.

The next message began to play. "Steven, this is Weber. Please fax the proposal letter after reviewing it with Ms. Rodriguez. Some minor adjustments might be needed before we send it out. Thanks."

Steven groaned internally. Of course. Fax. Mr. Weber, his old-school boss, still preferred the reliability of a fax machine over the efficiency of email. He quickly jotted down the note before deleting this message as well. Hanging up the phone, disappointment took over him.

All he wanted was a single message, a *single word* from Lisa.

The company car pulled up to the entrance of his hotel. Steven thanked the driver with a forced smile and stepped out into the warm evening air.

Reaching his room, he tossed his briefcase onto the bed with a sigh. The exhaustion from the long day was starting to settle in, but his mind refused to shut down. The unanswered call from Lisa nibbled at him, each passing minute fueling his anxieties. He tried to push the thoughts away, focusing on the upcoming weekend with Sophia, but the image of Lisa, or perhaps Lisa and Peter together, kept curling through his mind.

Frustrated, Steven decided to take a shower, attempting to distract himself. As his anger towards Peter eased, thoughts of work and his promotion started to surface. While everything seemed to be going smoothly, Steven knew he had to stay cautious—especially when it came to Drake.

Over the years, Drake made no secret of his desire to climb the corporate ladder, and Steven knew he wouldn't hesitate to use any means necessary. He knew Drake's weaknesses and knew what could ruin his image with Jada. Steven clenched his fists. Letting the cool water run over his head, he stood still for a moment, allowing it to wash away the persistent frustration. Slowly, he reached for the soap and lathered it in his hands, feeling the uneasiness slip from his mind.

Steadily, the whole day went by, and there was still no news from her. He knew he should call her again, but a strange blend of smugness and apprehension held him back. He sank onto the bed, the plush comfort offering little reprieve. He was caught in a web of his own making, his professional life blurring with the cracks in his personal life.

Exhaustion finally began to win over his anxieties, and Steven drifted off to sleep, an uneasy slumber interspersed by fragmented dreams.

But even sleep couldn't offer a complete escape. Peter's earlier voicemail kept nagging at him, a persistent itch in the back of his mind. Finally, surrendering to the quiet insistence, Steven reached for his phone. With a deep breath, he dialed Peter's number.

"Hello, Peter?" Steven straightened up on the bed as Peter answered the call.

"Hey, Steven," a groggy voice mumbled through the receiver. "Do you have any idea what time it is? Let a man sleep in peace."

Steven chuckled, the sound strained. "Yeah, I know it's late, buddy. Sorry to bother you, but I saw your missed call earlier. You said you needed to talk?"

"Nah, nothing that important," Peter yawned audibly. "Just wanted to catch up and see how things were going with you. It could definitely wait until the morning."

"Oh, I thought it might be something urgent," Steven said. He hesitated, then blurted out, "You know how these things go, right? Work gets stressful, keeps you up at night..." He trailed off, hoping to draw Peter out.

"Yeah, I hear you," Peter said vaguely. There was a long pause, filled only with static on the line. He could practically feel Steven's hesitation radiating through the phone.

Finally, Peter cut him off, his voice laced with concern. "What's going on, Steven? You don't sound quite yourself. Where are you, and why aren't you sleeping?"

"Uh, yeah, I'm alright. Just have a bit of a sore throat keeping me up. I'm at home, of course. Why wouldn't I be?"

Peter knew Steven well enough to recognize the lie. He took a deep breath, then decided to take a gamble. "Actually, Peter," he began, his voice low, "it's Lisa."

"Lisa? What about Lisa?"

"I think... I think she's seeing someone else," Steven blurted out, the words tumbling out in a rush.

"Whoa, hold on a minute," Peter said, his voice regaining some of its usual composure. "Why would you think that?"

Steven's frustration mounted. "Forget that. Do you know anything about this?"

This was it. The moment of truth.

Here was Peter's chance to unburden himself and confess everything to Steven, his best friend since childhood. He could blurt it all out: the stolen moments with Lisa, the whispered secrets, and the guilt that had been slowly consuming him from the inside out. But the words wouldn't come. The silence stretched on the phone line, heavy and thick with unspoken accusations.

Steven's voice finally broke through the tension.

"If she was cheating on me and you knew, would you honestly tell me?" Steven pressed.

"What? What are you even—"

"For Christ’s sake, just answer, Peter."

"Steven, that's a senseless question. You're my best friend, my buddy. You know I wouldn't do that to you." His voice, however, lacked its usual conviction, a wavering note that sent a sliver of doubt through Steven.

Steven didn't respond immediately. Peter could practically hear him on the other end, dissecting Peter's words, searching for any telltale sign of deceit. The silence stretched on, each passing second an eternity for Peter. He squeezed his eyes shut, hoping the lie would stick, silently counting on the crackling phone connection to hide the uncertainty in his voice. A bead of sweat trickled down his temple, the cool air from the air conditioner doing little to quell the rising panic within him.

"Oh really, Peter? Is that so?" Steven investigated.

The wariness that had been boiling behind the facade of their conversation finally bubbled over.

Peter's heart lurched. "Listen, Steven, if I knew anything at all about Lisa, you'd be the first person I'd tell. We go way back, remember? Like brothers, practically."

He forced a laugh, the sound brittle and unconvincing even to his own ears. A heavy silence followed, scattered only by the static on the line. "Steven, did you hear me?" Peter pressed, a tremor of fear creeping into his voice.

"I hear you, Peter," Steven finally replied; however, his words offered little comfort. "But I'll unearth every last detail. I am in Mexico right now, but I assure you, no stone will be left unturned, my friend." His tone forsook no room for argument. It was a clear declaration of intent, a promise that sent shivers down Peter's spine.

The words felt like a punch to the gut, a direct challenge that sent a jolt of terror through him. For a moment, he felt speechless. He knew, with a sickening certainty, that Steven wouldn't stop until he extracted the truth and the web of lies Peter had spun began to unravel.

Desperate to deflect the suspicion, Peter grabbed at the first straw he could clutch.

"Why are you in Mexico anyway?" he asked as he tried to shift the focus of the conversation.

"Business trip," Steven replied curtly.

"How long will you be there?" Peter pressed, his questions in a thinly veiled attempt to gather information to gauge the potential threat Steven posed.

Steven's silence stretched on for a beat too long. "Not entirely sure yet," he said vaguely. "But you can bet we'll pick up this conversation when I return." The casual threat in his words was unmistakable, a clear indication that this conversation was far from over.

Trying to salvage whatever remained of the conversation, Peter forced a light tone.

"Well, if you need anything at all while you're down there, Steven, don't hesitate to call," he chirped.

"I will," Steven replied curtly. There was a long pause, and Peter could practically hear him wrestling with his emotions on the other end of the line. "Listen, sorry for bothering you with a call so late. You get some rest."

"No worries, Steven," Peter mumbled as Steven finally seemed ready to end the call. "You too, and hey," he added, "just a heads up— those tacos down in Mexico can be pretty wild. Keep an eye out, alright?"

Steven didn't respond to Peter's last remark.

Right, because the biggest danger in Mexico is a rogue taco, he thought.

He forced a humorless chuckle, the kind that came more from habit than humor, at Peter's so-called "helpful travel advice." Every minute on the phone felt like he was walking a tightrope over a pit of vipers, and Steven was desperate to get off. Finally, with a click, the call ended.

Steven had hung up.

Peter stared at the phone in his hand, a dull ache blooming in his gut. He knew this was just the beginning. The truth, like a ticking time bomb, waited to explode, and Peter could only wait with bated breath for the inevitable fallout.

Meanwhile, on the other side of the phone line, Steven stared at the dark screen. The silence screamed with unspoken accusations, leaving a bitter taste in Steven's mouth.

At that moment, a seed of doubt about the very foundation of friendship took root in his mind.

Friendships...do they ever hold any real importance? What price are we willing to pay for them, if any at all? He thought bitterly.

Steven's suspicion towards Lisa only intensified after his conversation with Peter. He tossed the phone onto the bed with a frustrated sigh. His gaze glided towards the window, where the cityscape glittered with a thousand tiny lights.

Reaching for his phone once more, he bypassed the familiar contact and dialed a different number, going straight to voicemail.

"Mr. Patty, I apologize for the late call, but this is an urgent matter. I need you to find out everything you can about someone. Money is no object. Consider this a top priority." He rattled off the details in a businesslike manner.

He shut the phone with a click and took a deep breath, trying to quell the storm of emotions rampant within him.

Pushing aside the phone, Steven forced himself to focus on the stack of folders beside him. Meetings loomed in the morning, demanding his attention. He flipped open the first folder and looked through the documents within. But the words blurred before his eyes, lost in the fog of suspicion and betrayal.

With a sigh, he closed the folder and thought to himself, *I would get to the bottom of this, no matter the cost.*

Chapter 13: Dead End

The past two weeks had been a whirlwind for Drake. Ever since his last awkward encounter with Lisa, his thoughts had been swirling in a chaotic mix of regret and a yearning to make things right. He'd seen the dark circles under her eyes, the way her smile faltered when he mentioned Steven's sudden trip to Mexico.

It was clear that she was hurting—just like him.

Determined to mend fences, Drake decided to pull out all the stops. Antonio's—Lisa's absolute favorite restaurant—as she had mentioned earlier in one of their conversations, was the obvious choice. But snagging a reservation there was like trying to win the lottery. It was a celebrity hotspot, a place where tables were booked up months in advance.

Drake, however, wasn't easily deterred. He spent the next few days strategically placing calls, leveraging every last connection he had in the city. Drake wasn't above playing the "six degrees of separation" game to secure that coveted table.

However, getting the reservation was one thing; convincing Lisa to come was another. He needed her to understand his apology, to see that his intentions were sincere. Taking a deep breath, he dialed a number on his phone, hoping this would be the step that brought them back from the brink.

As the phone rang, Drake leaned back in his chair, hands clasped together. Every ring felt like an eternity, his anxiety building with each passing second. Finally, a friendly voice answered on the other end.

"Antonio's, this is Isabella speaking; how can I help you?"

"Hi Isabella, it's Drake," he greeted warmly. He knew Isabella well, the charming receptionist who always greeted him with a smile. Today, however, he needed more than just a friendly welcome.

"Drake! How lovely to hear from you," Isabella's voice chimed through the receiver. "What can I do for you today?"

"Well, Isabella," Drake began. "I was wondering if, by any chance, you might have a table for two available tomorrow night?"

A moment of silence followed his request. Drake could practically hear Isabella's smile falter on the other end.

"Oh, Drake, I'm so sorry," Isabella sighed apologetically. "We're completely booked tomorrow. Saturday nights are always our busiest."

Disappointment brimmed in Drake, a bitter taste in his mouth. He'd come so far, only to hit a dead end. But giving up wasn't an option. Lisa deserved a grand gesture, and Antonio's was the perfect setting.

"I know this is a long shot, Isabella, but is there absolutely nothing you can do? This is really important." he continued in a persuasive tone.

Then, with a sigh, Drake heard the telltale sound of fingers tapping on a keyboard.

"Alright, Drake, this is just for you, and I mean this literally. Don't tell anyone, but I might be able to squeeze a table for two tomorrow night. But if anyone finds out I did this, my head will be on a platter," Isabella finally conceded.

Relief flooded Drake's system, and a triumphant grin stretched across his face. "Isabella, you are a lifesaver!" he exclaimed. "You won't regret this, I promise."

"We'll see," Isabella chuckled.

"Now, to make this even more perfect," Drake continued, his mind already racing with the next step, "could you arrange for a flower delivery to Lisa Blackman's store tomorrow at noon? A beautiful bouquet, something that screams 'special occasion.'"

"Mrs. Blackman? Oh, she's a lovely lady," Isabella gushed, clearly a fan of Lisa. "Always so kind and gracious. Consider it done. Anything else I can help you with?"

"Yes, actually," Drake added. "With the flowers, could you include a card that simply says 'Dinner at 8 p.m.' with a question mark at the end?"

"Just 'Dinner at 8 p.m.'?" Isabella echoed.

"Exactly," Drake confirmed. "A little mystery never hurt anyone, right?"

Before Isabella could offer any further questions, Drake ended the call with a quick "Thanks again, Isabella! You're the best!"

A satisfied sigh bolted his lips. Everything was set. Now, all hc had to do was wait for Lisa's response. Would she accept his invitation, his carefully crafted olive branch? Only time would tell. He rocked back and forth in his chair, a nervous energy coursing through him.

He'd taken a gamble, but for Lisa, it was a risk he was more than willing to take.

***

Lisa slumped deeper into the couch, the dim light of the television casting dancing shadows across her face. The remote control felt heavy in her hand, the channels blurring together as she flipped through them with a mindless riffle of her wrist. Her stomach roiled with a knot of anxiety. Every unanswered text, every silent hour, felt like another piece of evidence piling up against her.

She knew Steven was still angry. However, she'd clung to the desperate hope that a heartfelt prayer, a whispered request into the night, would somehow bring him back.

But God, it seemed, wasn't working on her timetable.

With a sigh that condensed her worries, Lisa finally forced her attention back to the screen. A movie she vaguely recognized sputtered to life, the opening scene a montage of bustling cityscapes. Maybe a good distraction was exactly what she needed. She settled back and tried to focus on the plot, the details blurring together in the fog of her worries.

But the effort was wasted. Barely a minute had passed when her hand reached for her phone, seemingly of its own accord. It felt cold against her palm as she unlocked it, a familiar routine playing out on autopilot. Her fingers tapped through the apps, landing with a soft click on the photo gallery.

There, nestled among a sea of selfies and travel pics, was a photo of Steven. A wave of bittersweet nostalgia hit her. He was perched on the edge of an airplane seat, a weary smile gracing his lips. The caption below simply read, "Long layover. Can't wait to get home." It was a picture he'd sent her during one of his many business trips, a small token of affection across the miles.

As she stared at the image, a memory surfaced. Their laughter echoed in her mind, the playful banter exchanged mere days before his unexpected departure. Back then, the silence that followed hadn't felt so deafening, the distance not so insuperable. Now, however, the picture served as a blunt reminder of the chasm that had grown between them, which seemed to widen with every passing moment.

A smile, however, tugged at the corner of her lips as she remembered the scene captured in the photo. Steven had finally boarded the plane after a hectic day of last-minute goodbyes and hurried packing. He'd squeezed her hand at the airport before leaving, his eyes crinkling at the corners in a genuine smile. They'd spent the next few minutes stealing kisses, whispering promises of a romantic getaway upon his return, a brief interlude in their busy lives.

The smile was short-lived, however; the harsh reality of the present quickly eclipsed the fleeting memory. The events of the past few days came crashing back, a tide of confusion and betrayal. A tear brimmed up in her eye, blurring the image on the screen. She quickly brushed it away, a gesture of insolence against the well of emotions threatening to spill over. Tears wouldn't solve anything, mend the broken trust, or bring Steven back. They were only a painful reminder of her current state of isolation.

Before Lisa knew it, she dialed Steven's number. Part of her knew he wouldn't answer, that this was a call fueled by hope more than reason. But the other part, the desperate, yearning part, craved even the faintest echo of his voice, a connection in this lonely silence.

She stared at the screen for a heart-stopping moment, a battle raging within her. Should she talk? Was she ready to face the avalanche of emotions that would inevitably follow? But before she could decide—

"Hello?" came a soft and familiar voice, sending a jolt through her system.

It was Steven. The sound of his voice was so close yet so distant. There was relief that he might hold the answers to the questions churning in her mind. But alongside it, there was an undercurrent of bitterness, reminding her of the silence that had stretched between them for the past few days.

For a moment, Lisa was frozen, her mind a tangled mess of thoughts and feelings. *Was this the end?* The realization hit her with a cold dread, followed by a surprising wave of insolence. If this was their final chapter, she wouldn't let it be written without a fight. She wouldn't go down without a struggle.

Taking a fortifying breath, Lisa forced herself to speak.

"Steven... I'm sorry," she began.

She stared blankly at the television screen, its colorful images an unadulterated dissimilarity to the emotional disorder within her.

"I just wasn't expecting you to answer my call."

Silence followed her words, and then Steven's voice filled the receiver again.

"I wasn't expecting your call now if I'm being honest," he admitted.

Lisa scoffed internally. *Yeah, right*, she thought.

Little did they know, they were both operating on the same wavelength: a desperate desire for connection, a desire to bridge the gap that had grown between them.

Steven had been replaying their last conversation in his head. The frustration slowly gave way to a concern for loneliness. So, when her call came, unexpected and out of the blue, he'd answered without hesitation. He just wanted to hear her voice, if only for a moment. The silence on the other end, however, was starting to stretch.

"Sounds like we both surprised each other, then," he said with amusement.

The tension seemed to ease a fraction momentarily.

Lisa took another steadying breath. "Right," she managed, forcing a laugh that sounded rather high-pitched.

Another stretch of silence followed. This time, it stretched on for far too long. Lisa found herself twisting the soft cotton of her shirt hem between her fingers, a nervous habit she hadn't indulged in since childhood. A sheen of sweat began to prickle on her palms, a physical manifestation of the anxiety twisting in her gut.

The silence on the other end of the line overextended into an infinity, disrupted only by the frantic tick-tock of the clock on her wall. Each passing second felt like a tiny hammer blow to her already fragile hope.

Finally, unable to bear the suspense any longer, she blurted out, "Is this... is this how it ends?"

"What?”

"Our marriage… is this how it’s supposed to end? Because it seems like you don’t want to talk it out."

"No, no, absolutely not," he stammered. "This is actually a good time to talk. I left you a few messages but assumed you didn't want to pick up."

Lisa couldn't stay still any longer. She straightened herself and walked towards the kitchen, circling the center island. Her bare feet slapped a restless pace against the cool hardwood floor. The sound echoed in the otherwise silent room.

"It's just…" she started, her voice barely a whisper over the self-inflicted noise, "I didn't know how to put everything into words."

A gentle smile played on Steven's lips. "Lisa, we've been married for too long for you to clam up on me now. You've always been the one to speak your mind, to be honest about your feelings. Why change that now?"

Lisa stopped pacing, her back hitting the cool surface of the counter with a soft thud. She took a deep, shaky breath, trying to calm the emotions inside her.

"You left, Steven," she said finally.

It wasn't an accusation but a simple statement of fact. Even through the phone line, Steven could hear the underlying pain she'd tried so hard to mask. Lisa could hear Steven's sharp breath on the other end of the line.

"You went to Mexico without a word. And I was worried sick," her voice trembled slightly. Tears pricked at the corners of her eyes, blurring her vision.

A long pause followed, filled only with the hum of the phone line.

Then, Steven's voice came, slow and measured. "Lisa, you're the one who left and didn't come home. I waited up all night, and when I woke up the next morning, you were gone."

Lisa winced, the memory sharp and painful.

"Okay, okay," she conceded quickly, the fight momentarily draining out of her. "You're right. I shouldn't have stormed out like that."

She ran a hand through her hair, defeat blending with the enduring hurt.

"There's no point in trying to justify my actions, is there?" she sighed. "I was wrong, Steven. I was wrong to leave, and I'm truly sorry."

Steven remained silent on the other end, and Lisa could practically feel him scrutinizing her words. Lisa bit her lip, unsure of what to say next. She wasn't sure how much Steven knew about her night or how much she was willing to reveal.

"Maybe by now I should know how to handle these situations better," she finally ventured.

The silence stretched again. Finally, Steven's voice cut through the tension.

"Okay, so where were you that night?" he asked in a clipped tone.

Lisa hesitated, surprised by the directness. How much did he know? How much was he willing to believe? Taking a deep breath, she forced the words out.

"I stayed at a hotel," she admitted quietly. "Steven, I was hurt, yes, but I was also wrong to leave."

Steven didn't respond immediately. He listened intently to the tremor in her voice, the raw vulnerability that peeked through. A trace of hope bloomed in his chest. Maybe this time would be different. He desperately wanted to believe her. Yet, a troublesome doubt loitered in the back of his mind. Something about the situation didn't quite sit right.

It was a crossroads.

He could choose to trust her completely, to accept her explanation at face value, or he could choose the more cautious path, the one that acknowledged the cracks in their foundation of trust. He wasn't sure which way to go. A part of him yearned to believe Lisa and rebuild the trust that had been fractured. But his vigilant side couldn't shake the feeling that something wasn't adding up.

"Lisa, I don't want to place all the blame on you. We both have a role to play in this mess." He paused, searching for the right words. "Maybe things have gotten so complicated over the years; maybe we've lost sight of what we truly mean to each other. Maybe..."

Lisa, unable to bear the suspense any longer, cut him off. "No, Steven! There's no *maybe* about it. We can't just throw away a lifetime of love and shared experiences!" she insisted with desperation.

Steven sighed, the sound heavy with weariness.

"I'm not saying we throw it all away," he clarified. But if we're going to give this another shot, it has to be built on complete honesty. Maybe even professional help," he suggested, the idea tasting bitter on his tongue. "Or maybe... maybe it's time to consider going our separate ways before the damage becomes irreparable."

Lisa's heart struck against her ribs. Steven's words sounded heavy with implicit accusations and a terrifying possibility.

Did he know about Peter and her past mistakes? Worse yet, did he suspect Drake, the one-night stand she'd desperately tried to forget? Was the entire thing just a test, a cruel game to see how far she was willing to betray their vows?

The room seemed to shrink around her, suffocating. This was a delicate tightrope walk between truth and deception. Every word she uttered held the potential to tip the scales, to determine the fate of their relationship. She had to choose carefully. Every word, every inflection, could be the difference between mending their splintered bond or shattering it completely.

Taking a deep breath, Lisa forced her voice to sound steady. "Steven, you know I've always been honest with you, and I always will be. If there's something specific that's bothering you, something you need to know, just ask."

A tense silence followed her words. Lisa could practically feel Steven weighing her sincerity through the phone line.

Finally, he spoke with a weariness that sent a shiver through her. "Now isn't the time for *that* conversation, Lisa. But when I get back, I expect complete honesty. *Everything*."

Lisa's stomach clenched. There was a finality in his voice that sent a jolt of panic through her.

"And that goes for you too, Steven, right?" she countered.

She refused to let him end the conversation on a one-sided power trip. This had to be a two-way street, a path paved with honesty for both of them.

Steven remained silent for a beat; then, a sigh traveled through the phone. Across the room, Lisa could almost picture him adjusting his collar, a subconscious gesture betraying his growing hindrance.

"I understand," he conceded finally. "But like I said, now isn't the time. I really have to go."

The clatter of a door opening resounded faintly in the background, interrupted by a muffled greeting.

Lisa felt a cold dread creep into her heart. This wasn't over. This was just the beginning of a much larger conversation.

Lisa, desperate to hold onto this fragile connection, couldn't help but voice her concern.

"Steven, why the rush? Earlier, you said now was a good time to talk."

She frowned, a furrow engraving itself between her brows. The prospect of him hanging up again was unsettling.

"There's a meeting I have to attend. I'm actually in the conference room right now, and people are starting to arrive."

Relief washed over Lisa, momentarily easing the knot of tension in her stomach. A meeting, a simple explanation.

"Oh, alright," she conceded. "Well, call me tomorrow then, okay?"

There was a moment of silence, and then Steven spoke again. "I will," he promised. Then, almost as an afterthought, he added, "Lisa, listen to me. I love you. I always have, and I always will."

His words hit her like a balm, soothing the raw ache in her heart. A million pounds seemed to lift from her chest.

"I love you too, Steven," she replied.

Maybe there was hope for them after all.

"And one more thing…things are going to change. Do you understand me?"

Lisa paused. She didn't quite grasp the full meaning yet, but the sincerity in his voice was undeniable.

"I think I do, but we can talk about it later," she managed.

Right now, all that mattered was that he was coming back.

"Okay," he agreed. "Bye, Lisa. I really do have to go now."

The line went dead, leaving Lisa standing alone in the quiet kitchen. Fear and uncertainty, but most prominently, a ray of hope blossomed within her.

The conversation had been far from easy, but at least they were talking. And for now, that was enough. She would wait for his call, for the continuation of their conversation, and brace herself for the unknown journey that lay ahead.

***

Lisa sat hunched over her laptop as the night took over. Every click of the mouse and every tap of the keyboard felt mechanical, her mind a million miles away from the bills and spreadsheets demanding her attention. The repeat of Steven's words haunted her, his veiled threats and cryptic pronouncements replaying on a loop in her mind. *Did he know?*

The question bothered her, a persistent worm burrowing deeper into her already roiling stomach. Though veiled, he'd sounded different and distant, but his accusations persisted around her. A cold sweat prickled on her skin. The only person who knew about her betrayal was Peter, the man with whom she'd indulged in a foolish affair.

Suddenly, the sterile glow of the laptop screen seemed suffocating. With a sigh, Lisa pushed herself back from the desk and rubbed her tired eyes. She couldn't focus on the billing work any longer. Her gaze darted around the room, finally landing on her phone on the coffee table. The decision to call Peter wasn't an easy one. He was a complication she didn't need right now, but a desperate hope flashed within her.

Maybe he knew something, something that could explain Steven's strange behavior.

Her finger wandered over the phone screen for a long moment before she pressed the call button. The first ring echoed in the silence of the room, and then Peter picked up.

"Peter?" Lisa's voice came out a hoarse whisper, blatantly conflicting with the forced calmness she'd tried to project.

There was no room for pleasantries now, only the growing fear and a desperate hope for answers.

"Lisa? I wasn't expecting your call," Peter's voice came through the receiver. "Everything alright?"

He didn't get a chance to finish. Lisa cut him off. "What have you been talking to Steven about? What's going on between you two?"

The question hung between them, interposed by the faint hum of traffic filtering through the phone line. A lump of anxiety constricted in Lisa's stomach. Surely, Peter wouldn't have been so careless, wouldn't have betrayed her trust so easily?

Across the line, Peter frowned. He'd just settled into his favorite armchair, a steaming mug of tea in hand, when Lisa's unexpected call startled him. Now, caught off guard by her accusatory tone, a hint of concern flashed in his eyes.

"What are you talking about? Maybe I misunderstood. We haven't spoken about anything important lately, have we? But listen, there's definitely nothing I'm keeping from you."

Lisa scoffed a harsh sound that scraped against his ear.

"Peter, listen to me carefully. This is important. Do you know anything about what Steven might be suspecting?"

Peter winced at the coldness in her tone. He could practically feel the distance between them crackle with tension. He squeezed his eyes shut for a moment, willing himself to stay calm.

"Whoa, Lisa, hold on a minute. What are you trying to imply here? Steven and I haven't spoken a word to each other."

The rational part of Peter hesitated. He didn't want to reveal too much, not yet. Letting Lisa in on the full truth could backfire if she decided to come clean to Steven first, casting him as the villain before he had a chance to explain himself.

Meanwhile, Lisa hesitated. Steven's indirect allegations resounded in her mind, fueling her paranoia.

"I don't understand. Steven just called, and everything feels different. He was asking me questions, and I can't help but feel like you might be involved somehow."

So, Steven suspected something? Peter thought. This was worse than he'd imagined.

"Lisa, this all sounds confusing. I honestly have no idea what Steven might be thinking," he hedged, stalling for time. "But there's something I need to tell you, something important. Can we talk about it soon?"

He hoped that by turning the conversation around, he could buy himself some time to figure out what was going on and, more importantly, assure Lisa that he hadn't betrayed her trust. But his carefully crafted plan crumbled before his ears.

"Peter, there's nothing left to discuss," came Lisa's voice with a quiet finality.

The distance between them now felt like a vast, uncrossable chasm.

"This has gone on for too long," she continued. "I can't keep doing this, Peter. It was a mistake, a terrible lapse in judgment from the beginning. We should have never..."

Before Peter could muster a response, Lisa pressed on. But this time, he wouldn't get a chance to hear her.

"Lisa, wait!" he interjected. "This isn't about that. We need to talk. Nothing else!" He closed his eyes, trying to calm his thundering heart. "I just found something out. Something that could change everything. We seriously need to talk."

But his words seemed to backfire. A choked sob escaped Lisa, a sound that sent a jolt of panic through Peter.

"No… No! I don't want to talk about it, Peter. Not now, not ever. Just leave me alone." The finality in her voice brooked no argument.

Frustration bubbled up within Peter. "This is important! I just need a few minutes, but not on the phone. It's complicated." he insisted.

Silence. Then, a single word shattered the tense atmosphere. "No," Lisa's voice was cold, devoid of warmth.

Before Peter could plead further, the dial tone pierced his ear. He stared at the phone in disbelief, the weight of her rejection settling heavily in his gut. Anger flared, quickly followed by a crushing despair. She wouldn't even listen. He had information, critical information, and she wouldn't give him a chance.

"Lisa! Lisa! Hello?" Peter stammered into the dead receiver, his voice echoing in the emptiness before he slammed the phone down.

The frustration crackled around him, thick enough to choke on. Peter knew that Lisa wouldn't be swept under the rug. He had to talk to her—face to face. Now, the question wasn't if, but how. He would find her, confront her, and make her understand. The truth, a tangled mess of consequences, wore him down. It was a ticking time bomb, and silence was no longer an option.

Chapter 14: Game of Chance

The afternoon sun formed a warm glow through the dusty windowpanes of Lisa's shop, illuminating a haven of tradition and forgotten treasures. Worn wooden shelves hugged the walls, groaning slightly under the weight of their squarely displayed contents. Here, hand-stitched quilts in vibrant patterns were folded neatly, their faded colors whispering stories of generations past. Gleaming brass candlesticks stood sentinel next to chipped porcelain teacups, each piece a testament to a bygone era.

Lisa moved with practiced ease amongst the familiar clutter. Her fingers, nimble and sure, traced the delicate embroidery of a lace tablecloth, her mind a three-ring-circus of emotions. The call with Peter had left her shaken, a tangled mess of unanswered questions and gnawing fear. Yet, as she reached for her inventory list, a sturdy tenacity settled in her eyes.

Taking a deep breath, Lisa perched on a creaky stool behind the counter. She took in the neatly organized columns of the list, each item a tangible reminder of the life she'd built. Porcelain dolls, vintage tins, and hand-blown glass ornaments were more than just merchandise; a livelihood she'd nurtured for years. But right now, they felt more like a shield, a barrier against the tempest infusing in her personal life.

With a new purpose, Lisa began ticking off items on the list, her pen scratching rhythmically on the paper. Each checkmark felt like a step toward securing her ground. Lisa knew that she wouldn't let fear paralyze her. She would fight to protect herself from the secrets and lies threatening to shatter the life she'd so carefully built.

A faint jingle of bells, the shop's gentle welcome chime, pierced the tense silence. Lisa's head snapped up, her gaze flitting from the completed list to the doorway. A man stood framed in the sunlight streaming through the dusty windowpanes, a cardboard box cradled in his arms.

A sliver of hope sparked in Lisa's chest for a fleeting moment. *Could it be...?*

But the hope died as quickly as it arose. The delivery man's uniform and the impersonal way he held the box made that unlikely. Still, a drop of curiosity remained.

"I'll be right there," Lisa announced.

She quickly entered the last digits of her credit card on the small keypad of the terminal beside her, her eyes lingering on the confirmation screen for a beat longer than necessary.

With a deep breath, she tapped "complete order" and pushed the receipt toward the counter's edge.

"Is that a delivery?" Lisa asked.

The delivery man grunted, with a clipboard in his hand. "Flowers for Mrs. Blackman," he mumbled, barely looking up.

Flowers? Lisa's heart skipped a beat.

"I'm Mrs. Blackman, but I wasn't expecting any flowers."

Her mind conjured images of senders both desired and dreaded. Surely, whoever sent these cared a great deal. The vibrant blooms overflowing from the box seemed to whisper promises and unspoken emotions.

"Was there a note indicating who they're from?" Lisa pushed.

The delivery man shrugged.

"There's a note, but I didn't read it. Can you sign here, please?" He tapped the clipboard with a bored expression.

Apparently, for him, this was just another delivery, another transaction.

Lisa scribbled her signature on the clipboard with a practiced hand, the memory of Peter's frantic call and Steven's veiled accusations whipping in her stomach.

As the delivery man turned to leave, the box brushed against his leg, momentarily revealing a riot of color and fragrance. Lisa couldn't help herself.

"Oh!" she gasped, a genuine smile replacing the professional one.

The sweet, heady aroma of lilies and roses filled the air, chasing away the shadows in her mind.

Flowers. A small, unexpected gesture that always managed to lift her spirits. The delivery man grunted in acknowledgment.

"Thank you. Have a nice day." Lisa said sincerely.

He mumbled a goodbye and shuffled toward the door. As it swung shut with a soft thud, Lisa carefully took the box from the counter. The intensity of it surprised her; a generous arrangement, she realized with a growing sense of keenness.

Placing the box on a nearby table, she peeled back the colorful wrapping paper, revealing a breathtaking display of lilies and roses, their delicate petals dusted with morning dew. A small white card nestled amongst the blooms caught her eye.

With shuddering fingers, she pulled it out and unfolded it. A single line of elegant script graced the card: *Dinner tonight, 8 p.m. at Antonio's?*

A wide smile bloomed on Lisa's face. Dinner at Antonio's could only mean one thing. Steven was home, and despite the secrets or lies he might be harboring right now, he clearly wanted to make things special. A wave of relief washed over Lisa, momentarily pushing aside the anxieties of the day.

A light, giddy feeling bubbled up inside her.

Perhaps a romantic dinner was exactly what we needed; maybe, amidst the candlelight and soothing music, we could finally clear the air and rebuild the trust that seemed so fragile, she thought to herself.

With a new lightness in her step, Lisa began to tidy the shop, humming a forgotten melody. She couldn't tear her gaze away from the vibrant blooms. Picking up the vase they came in, a standard glass container that clashed with their delicate beauty, a resolute decision formed in her mind.

Today wasn't about the daily grind. Today was about a fresh start, a chance to rewrite the narrative. Lisa carried the flowers to a dusty ceramic vase tucked away on a high shelf. It was her grandmother's, a pale blue adorned with delicate white flowers, a perfect match for the lilies and roses.

Carefully, she rearranged the stems, their colors bursting to life against the cool blue background. Freshwater glistened in the afternoon sun, mirroring the sudden sparkle in Lisa's eyes. An emotion she hadn't felt in a long time bubbled up within her: a heady mix of excitement and hope. The prospect of seeing Steven after their time apart, the promise of a romantic dinner, it all painted a picture of a future brighter than she'd dared to imagine lately.

A surge of energy coursed through her. The mundane tasks of inventory suddenly seemed insignificant. With a decisive flick of her wrist, Lisa locked the shop door earlier than usual. The golden light of the setting sun cast long shadows as she hurried down the street, a secret smile playing on her lips.

The scent of nail polish and acetone greeted her as she pushed open the door of her favorite salon. Inside, a cheerful melody danced through the air, disrupted by the whirring of electric nail files. Lisa felt a wave of nervous excitement envelop her. This wasn't just about a manicure; it was a small act of self-care, a way to prepare for the night ahead. She settled into the plush chair, the cool leather instantly relaxing her tense muscles.

As the nail technician, a young woman with bright red hair, began her work, Lisa scrolled through her phone on autopilot. Emails blurred before her eyes, their contents meaningless compared to the surge of emotions spinning inside her. Every few seconds, her gaze would flick down to her hands, a silent question in her eyes: *Are they done yet?*

With a satisfied nod, the nail technician presented Lisa with her newly painted nails: a classic shade of cherry red that gleamed under the salon lights. A feeling of completeness took over her. Tonight, she was ready to face Steven, a woman reborn with hope and a touch of red lacquer confidence. A silent vow formed in her heart: no matter what came of this evening, she would face it head-on. The anxieties that had nibbled at her for weeks seemed to melt away, replaced by a steely fortitude.

Reaching her home, Lisa practically skipped up the stairs to the bedroom. A glance at the clock sent a jolt of urgency through her. Time seemed to be moving at double speed as she raced through the rest of her pre-date routine. A refreshing shower washed away the day's stress, replaced by the refreshing scent of her favorite lavender soap.

Back in the bedroom, her steps quickened as she reached the closet; a battlefield of clothes suddenly transformed into a treasure trove of possibilities. She scanned the hanging garments, her fingers trailing over smooth silks and crisp pieces of cotton.

The perfect dress, she knew intuitively, wouldn't just be about looks. It needed to reflect the new Lisa, a woman ready for romance but also self-assured. A soft blue dress caught her eye, its color reminiscent of the clear summer sky after a storm. It would complement the red of her nails perfectly.

Pulling it out, she slipped it on, the fabric caressing her skin like a gentle breeze. Gazing into the mirror, she broke into a contented smile.

Lisa scanned the room one last time. A stray glance at the clock confirmed her worst fear: she was running late.

With a determined sigh, she grabbed her purse and dashed out the door, her steps echoing down the hallway. Reaching her car, she slid behind the wheel, a soft jazz station instantly filling the air. The familiar sounds of Kenny G brimmed the air around her, a calming melody that soothed her racing heart.

It was a perfect blend, she thought, a reflection of the night ahead. Exciting enough to keep the thrill high but also relaxed enough to savor every moment. Lisa pulled out of the driveway, her red taillights disappearing into the twilight, leaving behind a trail of hope and a woman ready to reclaim her love story.

Lisa pulled her car slowly into the bustling valet stand at Antonio's. As she came to a stop, a young man in a crisp uniform materialized at her door, a welcoming smile lighting up his face.

"Good evening, ma'am. Lovely car you have. I trust you're having a wonderful evening?" he greeted with a courteous bow.

Lisa offered a warm smile in return. "Yes, thank you."

"Well, I hope you continue to enjoy," the valet said, taking the keys she held out.

He expertly maneuvered the car out of sight, leaving Lisa feeling a flutter of eagerness in her stomach.

With a glance at her reflection in the nearby car's window, along with a final check to ensure her lipstick was perfectly in place, Lisa stepped out onto the sidewalk. The cool night air carried the scent of jasmine and freshly cut grass, a pleasant dissimilarity to the city's usual exhaust fumes.

Another young man, dressed in a smartly tailored dark grey suit, held the entrance door open for her. "Good evening, madam," he greeted politely.

"Thank you," Lisa replied, offering a grateful smile.

Stepping inside, she was met with a warm wave of energy. The restaurant buzzed with conversation and laughter, the soft glow of candlelight creating an intimate atmosphere.

The air itself seemed to vibrate with a low hum of music, a melody that instantly transported her back to countless romantic dinners shared with Steven. Her eyes moved around the room, searching for his familiar face amidst the sea of happy couples.

Just then, a young woman with a bright smile approached her. "Mrs. Blackman?" she inquired. "Lovely to see you. Let me show you to your table."

"Thank you," she replied, stepping forward. "Is my host here yet?"

"Yes, he is already waiting," the receptionist confirmed, gesturing towards the dining area. "Just follow me this way."

Lisa's heart struck frantically in her chest. With each step closer, the promise of a long overdue conversation seemed to envelop her.

Finally, the hostess stopped in front of a secluded table tucked away in a quiet corner. The flaming candlelight projected a warm glow on a single red rose to rest in a crystal vase, a perfect symbol of the romantic evening Lisa envisioned.

"Can I get you something to drink while you are waiting?"

Lisa's smile hesitated slightly. "White wine, please," she replied, the disappointment momentarily clouding her excitement.

"Of course, ma'am," the hostess chirped, disappearing into the bustling restaurant.

Left alone, Lisa reached into her purse, pulling out a small compact mirror. One last check to ensure her lipstick was perfectly in place, a final act of self-assurance before facing Steven.

Suddenly, a shadow fell across the table, accompanied by the sound of a chair scraping against the floor. Lisa's heart leaped into her throat. She looked up, expecting to see Steven's face.

Instead, she was met with a sight that sent a jolt of icy fear through her veins.

It was Drake.

He was the last person Lisa wanted to see, especially here, at a table meant for her and Steven. The carefully constructed image of a romantic evening shattered in an instant. Panic scratched at her throat, stealing her breath away.

"Drake? What are you doing here?"

A sly smile spread across Drake's face, his eyes staying on her a touch too long for comfort.

"Well, Lisa, isn't this your favorite restaurant? Or at least, that's what you said," he drawled.

He lowered himself into the chair opposite her. Leaning back, he propped his leg casually on the chair next to him, the very picture of misplaced confidence.

Lisa felt nausea rise in her stomach.

"Please, Drake, just leave. Steven is here, and I really don't want anything to upset him," she pleaded.

Drake looked around the restaurant with a slow, unsettling grin. A harsh laugh erupted from his lips, coupled with a hint of mockery.

"Oh, you think this whole charade was Steven's doing? No, my dear Lisa. Steven's still enjoying his 'little vacation' in Mexico. This little surprise? All me," he drawled.

Lisa's heart felt like a trapped bird desperate for escape. The oh-so-perfect evening was replaced by a scene straight out of her worst nightmare.

"What are you talking about?" she demanded. "Steven and I come here all the time. This isn't funny, Drake."

Panic surged through her veins, a cold sweat prickling her skin. The familiar warmth of the restaurant suddenly felt suffocating.

"I just thought it would be a nice gesture, you know? A chance to make amends for my previous transgression."

A trace of memory sparked in Lisa's mind when Drake visited last. Anger flared shortly, quickly dowsed by overwhelming anxiety.

"I thought Steven was back, and we were going to…"

The image of a candlelit dinner with Steven, a night filled with reconciliation and rekindled love, felt like a cruel mirage. Rising abruptly from her chair, she grabbed her purse, the need to escape overwhelming.

"But I didn't know!" Drake exclaimed. He lunged forward, his hand reaching out to grab her arm.

"Don't touch me!" Lisa cried, swatting his hand away with a force that surprised even her.

The delicate balance she'd held all evening, the nervous hope for a fresh start with Steven, had shattered into a million pieces.

The last thing she needed was a scene, not here, not in her favorite restaurant, where everyone knew her face. She cast a frantic glimpse around the room.

"I have to get out of here. This isn't right, and I don't want anyone to get the wrong idea," she muttered.

The arrival of the hostess with Lisa's white wine momentarily arrested her escape.

"Your glass of wine, ma'am," she chirped, placing it carefully on the table.

Her gaze, however, fluctuated between Lisa and Drake, a furrow creasing her brow. The sight of Drake's hand, still hovering possessively near Lisa's arm, clearly caused her some confusion.

"Can I get you anything else?" she inquired.

Lisa, caught between her desperate desire to leave and a sudden aversion to creating a scene, felt helplessness rise inside her.

Images of well-known faces flashed through her mind: the regulars at the bar who always greeted her with a warm smile, the friendly manager who knew her order by heart. The thought of them witnessing a public display with Drake was a horrifying prospect.

With a forced smile and a voice laced with a tremor she couldn't quite control, Lisa replied, "No, thank you!" Her words were directed at the hostess, but her eyes remained fixed on Drake.

The young woman, seemingly sensing the tension, offered a curt nod before turning to address another table. Relief brimmed Lisa, fleeting but real.

"Drake, whatever you think this is, it isn't going to work. You know that, don't you?"

He simply leaned back in his chair, a smug smile twisting his lips. "Maybe it isn't," he replied, his words more infuriating than comforting.

Lisa breathed a shaky sigh of reprieve. At least he wasn't delusional enough to believe she'd leave Steven for him. But what, then, was his endgame?

"But you have two choices here—either you can get up and leave, upset and drawing everyone's attention. Or, you could have a drink and some dinner with me, like…old friends."

The last part was delivered with a mocking emphasis, and the implication was clear. He knew he had her cornered.

Lisa's finely done nails dug into her palms. She hated that he was right. Leaving now would only fuel gossip and speculation.

With a deep breath, she forced herself to relax, a mask of indifference replacing the storm of emotions steeping beneath the surface. Picking up the wine glass, she took a small, reluctant sip, the tart liquid offering little comfort.

Tonight, it seemed, her romantic evening had been hijacked by an unwelcome guest and his twisted sense of amusement. However, despite feeling trapped, Lisa wasn't one to give up without a fight. This game of cat and mouse had just begun, and she, unlike Drake, still held a few cards close to her chest. Or at least, that's what she hoped.

Chapter 15: Double Trouble

The opulent interior of Antonio's Restaurant was bathed in a warm, golden glow from dimmed crystal chandeliers. Lush greenery cascaded down ornately carved pillars, creating secluded intimacy within the gentle murmur of conversation. The air vibrated with the soft strains of a jazz quartet, casting a spell of sophistication and romance.

However, the ambiance did little to mask the hollowness Lisa felt tonight.

Perched on the edge of a plush velvet chair, she found herself acutely aware of the stark contrast between the luxurious setting and the confusion churning within her. Drake sat across the table, his presence a jarring dissonance in this haven of elegance.

His gaze, equal parts amusement and something more predatory lingered on her a beat too long before finally breaking away.

"White wine, a classic choice," he remarked with feigned casualness. "Funny, I was just about to order the same for you."

Lisa remained silent, her response a studied indifference. She observed him from above the rim of her glass with a silent challenge in her eyes. Each sip of the wine was a calculated move, a way to buy herself time, to formulate a plan.

"But then again, it seems I know your favorite restaurant better than just its ambiance. Let's say your particular choices are also a familiar territory," Drake continued.

A knot of tension tightened in Lisa's gut. What was his endgame here? Was he simply trying to rekindle a connection long extinguished, or was there something more sinister at play?

"What point are you trying to make, Drake?" she finally asked.

Drake draped one leg over the other, the picture of misplaced confidence.

"Just saying, Lisa," he drawled, his eyes never leaving hers, "that perhaps I know you a little better than your husband might."

The audacity of his statement sent a jolt of anger through Lisa. How dare he, this self-absorbed relic from her past, make such a claim?

"Oh God, Drake," she scoffed, a touch of exasperation creeping into her voice. "You don't even know…"

Drake, sensing her hesitation, seized the opportunity to press his point. "Don't know what, Lisa?" he inquired. "That you're not exactly picture-perfect happy with your marriage?"

Lisa hesitated, the clinking of silverware and hushed conversations providing a comforting backdrop to her internal struggle.

"Drake," she began carefully, "Steven and I are working through some things. We've talked openly about them, and…" She trailed off, searching for the right words.

There was a vulnerability to Drake's question that caught her off guard. She wanted to confide in him, to explain the cracks in her marriage that seemed to be growing wider, but the weight of her vows held her back.

"Everything?" Drake interjected. "So, he knows about us?"

A flicker of anger sparked in his eyes, his jaw clenching slightly. Here he was, attempting a grand romantic gesture, and Lisa was throwing water on the flames with talk of marital problems. It felt like a slap in the face.

"There is no 'us,' Drake," Lisa countered. "What happened was a momentary lapse, a mistake."

Drake let out a humorless chuckle, its sound echoing oddly in the luxurious space. He could see the turmoil in Lisa's expression and the way she weighed her options with each passing moment. The anger threatened to boil over again, but he forced it down.

He wouldn't chase her away with displays of temper. No, Drake had a plan, a carefully constructed one that would ensure they ended up together. One that would completely destroy Steven Blackman, and what better way to do it than by winning over his wife?

Leaning closer, his voice dipped to a murmur, "Lisa, you can't deny the spark. You enjoyed yourself, and now you're calling it a mistake? I think you're misconstruing things." His eyes held a glint of challenge. "Look, I apologize for showing up at your house unannounced. It was a lapse in judgment, but what's done is done." He spoke with a finality that surprised Lisa.

Was he giving her an out, a chance to retreat with a shred of dignity?

"This isn't how apologies work, Drake. You used—" Her retort was cut short by the arrival of a cheerful waitress, her presence a jarring interruption.

"Good evening. Are you two ready to order? We have some amazing specials tonight. The lobster thermidor is simply divine, or perhaps you'd prefer the rack of lamb marinated in rosemary and garlic? We also have a delightful seared tuna steak with a citrus and caper sauce."

"Thank you," Lisa said quickly, stealing a glance at Drake. "We could use a few more minutes, please."

The waitress beamed. "Of course, just take your time. May I offer you a drink, sir?"

"Dry martini, please," Drake replied, his voice smooth as silk. "And when you come back, we should be ready."

He cast Lisa a pointed look, a silent reminder of the audience they now had. It was a clever move, Lisa realized with a pit in her stomach. If she bolted now, the attentive waitress would surely notice, and the next time she walked into Antonio's with Steven, it could become a scene—all thanks to Drake's calculated play.

The waitress beamed. "Good choice, sir. The martinis here are top-notch."

As she bustled away, Drake leaned back in his chair, a triumphant smirk playing on his lips.

"So, Lisa, what will it be? Dinner and a chance to clear the air or a dramatic exit that leaves the staff wondering what just happened?" He paused, then added, "Honestly, I think you should stay. Picture this: me, sitting here alone, regaling the waitress with tales of our...*acquaintance*. Not exactly the image you want to project, is it?"

His eyes gleamed with a calculated innocence.

Lisa's jaw clenched. She could practically see the gears turning in Drake's mind, the sly smile on his face a dead giveaway that he was up to something. *But what?*

He was playing his cards close to his chest, leaving her feeling like a pawn.

"Just dinner," she finally conceded. "No dessert and absolutely nothing more."

"Good choice. Perhaps you could decide on your meal before the waitress returns. We wouldn't want to keep her waiting all night, would we?"

Lisa offered a curt nod, her shoulders slumped in defeat. All she wanted was to put this entire evening behind her, to be back home, safe and sound, with Steven by her side.

With a sigh, she twisted a loose thread on her dress, her fingers working unconsciously.

"Honestly, Drake, I've lost my appetite entirely. Maybe just a salad," she muttered.

"Come on, didn't the lobster thermidor sound divine? It's practically their signature dish," Drake wheedled, raising his arm, a practiced move to flag down the waitress who, as if on cue, materialized beside them.

Lisa flinched inwardly. Drake's relentless pursuit was starting to grate on her nerves. She forced a weak smile at the waitress.

"Actually, I'll have the lobster thermidor, please." It felt like a surrender, a concession to the charade they were enacting.

"Excellent choice! And for you, sir?" the waitress inquired, gesturing toward Drake.

"The rack of lamb, medium rare, please," Drake replied.

The meal arrived, a feast for the eyes on pristine white plates. For Lisa, the food held little appeal; Drake, however, seemed determined to make conversation.

"So, tell me," he began, spearing a piece of lamb, "how's the shop doing?"

"Fine," Lisa mumbled, taking a small bite of her salad.

"Fine? Just fine? Come on, Lisa, a little detail wouldn't hurt."

"There's nothing to tell," she said curtly, pushing the plate away slightly.

Drake persisted, a glint in his eyes. "Wow, did you get your nails done recently? That color is fantastic." He leaned closer, trying to catch a better look.

Lisa instinctively curled her fingers into fists, hiding the polish underneath. This wasn't about Steven anymore; it was about maintaining a shred of privacy, a tiny piece of herself that wasn't entangled in this awkward situation.

"It's old," she lied, staring down at her lap.

Drake's smile faltered for a moment, but he quickly recovered.

"Well, it looks lovely," he said, albeit with less conviction. He offered her a piece of lamb from his plate. "Here, try some of this. It's really good."

Lisa shook her head, her voice barely audible. "No, thank you."

Each word felt heavy, laden with implicit anxieties. The glamorous setting and expensive meal—all felt hollow to Lisa. She felt trapped, a fly caught in the web of Drake's carefully spun evening. His questions and stanch stare all felt suffocating. Each monosyllabic response seemed to irritate him further.

Here he was, seemingly in control, yet she refused to play his game. All she wanted was for this charade to end, to escape this gilded cage and return to the normalcy of her life.

The frustration rumbling behind the frontage finally boiled over. Drake slammed his napkin onto the table with a sharp crack, the sound echoing in the opulent silence. He wiped his mouth with a flourish.

"Alright, Lisa. Since conversation seems to be a lost cause, let's cut to the chase. I'd like coffee and dessert, and then..." He paused. His smile, once charming, now held a dangerous edge. "...I expect you to come with me to my place. We can finish the night there."

Lisa's breath tethered in her throat. His words struck her like a physical blow, the anger that had been seething now blazing in his eyes. For a moment, she was speechless, stunned by the audacity of his proposition.

"Drake, are you *crazy*? Haven't you been listening to a word I've said?"

Drake rested back in his chair, a smug smile playing on his lips.

"Oh, I heard you alright, Lisa. But let's be honest here. You're not exactly picture-perfect marriage material these days, are you? We both know the truth. And the truth is, this night wouldn't be complete without us...finishing what we started." He winked, his gaze lingering suggestively on her.

Lisa felt a rush of nausea rise in her throat. Here it was, laid bare. The truth he spoke of wasn't some grand revelation but a self-serving fantasy he'd constructed in his mind. She thumped her napkin onto the table with a resounding thud. With a jerk, she pushed back her chair and stood, her body trembling with anger and disgust.

"You are unbelievable, Drake. Every single thing Steven said about you is true. Why are you doing this to me? Why can't you just accept that I'm not interested?" she spat, her voice rising with every syllable, drawing the attention of nearby diners who exchanged curious glances.

The commotion didn't go unnoticed.

The waitress hurried over. "Mrs. Blackman, is everything alright? Was there a problem with the lobster thermidor?"

Lisa took a deep breath, forcing a semblance of calm. "No, thank you, everything was lovely. I just need to excuse myself for a moment to go to the restroom."

Before Lisa could fully turn away, Drake interjected. "Actually, we'd like to finish off the meal with some coffee and dessert. Perhaps the cheesecake? Is it as good as the reviews online suggest?"

He flashed the waitress a charming smile.

The waitress, momentarily flustered by Drake's sudden attentiveness, stammered slightly. "Oh, the cheesecake, sir? It's absolutely divine! Made fresh daily with a light, fluffy crust and a creamy, decadent filling. You won't regret it, I assure you."

With a curt nod of thanks, Drake turned back to Lisa, a triumphant smirk playing on his lips. Lisa, however, remained silent, her jaw clenched tight. She mumbled a quick excuse about the restroom and retreated, her hurried steps echoing in the opulent silence.

The waitress, sensing the tension, stayed for a moment. "Would you like one slice or two for dessert, sir?" she inquired cautiously.

"One will suffice for now," Drake replied, his eyes moving towards the bathroom entrance. "I'm confident it'll be plenty to share if she decides she'd like some." He paused, then added, "And a black coffee, please. Strong."

The waitress nodded and hurried away to fulfill his order. After what felt like more than just a few minutes, Lisa emerged from the restroom; her dress smoothed down as if to erase any outward signs of her internal turmoil. A glimpse at their table revealed the waitress setting down a single slice of cheesecake and a steaming cup of coffee. Lisa sat back down heavily, tapping her foot impatiently against the floor. Each tick of her shoe seemed to reverberate the question that echoed in her mind: *How could she escape this situation unscathed?*

As the waitress left, Lisa steeled her nerves and leaned forward. "Drake, why are you putting me through this? What have I ever done to you?"

A cruel smile played on Drake's lips.

"Oh, Lisa, you really think this is about you? Naive, as always. I'm surprised you haven't figured it out yet." He leaned closer. "This is about Steven. Your squeaky-clean husband doesn't deserve the position he holds or the power he wields. He certainly doesn't deserve you." A bitter edge crept into his voice. "But some things are simply out of reach, wouldn't you agree?"

He almost spat the last words out, his eyes flashing with barely contained animosity. Apparently, even for his grand plan, getting thrown out of Antonio's wasn't part of the equation.

Lisa recoiled, her blood running cold. "If you have a problem with Steven, that's for the two of you to handle. You led me to believe he was something he wasn't. I *trusted* you."

"Ha! Trusted me?" Drake scoffed. "You chose to believe what suited your fancy. Convenient, wasn't it? To ignore the truth and paint Steven as some kind of saint. Well, the truth is, I haven't changed. I'm the same person I—"

Their tense exchange was abruptly cut short again by the arrival of the ever-attentive waitress. "May I get you anything else this evening?" she inquired politely.

"Actually, yes," Drake said smoothly.

He pushed his untouched coffee cup towards the waitress, a pointed look in his eyes. "This one seems to have gone cold. Could I trouble you for a fresh cup, nice and hot this time?"

The request, delivered with a calm authority that spoke volumes, effectively silenced Lisa and left the waitress scurrying away to fulfill it.

Her smile, previously bright and friendly, faltered slightly. She cast a quick glance at Lisa, whose face was a mask of barely concealed anger, and then at Drake, who seemed momentarily stunned. Without a word, she grabbed the coffee mug and retreated hurriedly, the unspoken message clear: *she understood the situation required a swift exit.*

Lisa watched her go, defeat nibbling at her like a persistent ache. Across from her, Drake, ignorant to the undercurrent of tension, casually speared a bite of cheesecake with his fork.

"Can we just finish this dessert and get out of here?" Lisa finally blurted out. "I really don't want to be here any longer."

Drake, mid-chew, paused and offered a sly smile. "So, you are coming with me after all?" He took a large bite of cheesecake, leaving the question hanging in the air.

"Coming with you? *Absolutely not.* I just want to leave."

"Well, you know things haven't exactly been… pleasant for me as well. I was hoping to have a word with a few people at the office and clear the air a bit."

Lisa felt a prickle of sweat crawl down her spine. *No, no, no. Taking this to the office meant unleashing a wildfire of gossip, the news spreading like wildfire until it reached Steven's ears*. The consequences were unthinkable.

"Drake, please," she pleaded. "You can't say anything! Promise me. I haven't done anything wrong. I'm sorry about how you feel about Steven, but—"

"*Sorry?* Lisa, you're the one who initiated this whole thing. Remember, you were the one who practically dragged me to your table. Couldn't resist my charm, could you?" (He approached her)

A victorious twinkle sparked in his eyes. He was winning this twisted game, and he wasn't about to let her forget it.

Lisa's cheeks burned with anger and humiliation. "You are a complete and utter idiot!" she spat.

Drake threw his hands up in mock surrender. "Whoa there, easy. So, you're saying it's all my fault? Don't make me regret taking you to dinner tonight, sweetheart."

Lisa, fuming, waved her hand dismissively. The waitress appeared instantly, sensing the shift in the atmosphere.

"Can we get the bill, please? And quickly," Lisa said.

"No problem, ma'am," the waitress replied, her smile strained. "I'll be right back."

"You know, you're actually kind of attractive when you're mad. Adds a little spice, you know?" Drake gritted his teeth.

Lisa rose abruptly. Ignoring Drake's protests, she dug into her purse and pulled out a wad of cash. Sitting there waiting for him to pay felt like an eternity, an additional torture she simply wasn't willing to endure.

"Hey! What are you doing?" Drake sputtered, surprised by her sudden action.

"We've created enough drama for one night," Lisa retorted.

The waitress reappeared, the bill in hand. Lisa snatched it from her grasp, shoved a generous amount of cash inside the folder, and practically ran for the door. Drake, momentarily stunned, scrambled to follow her.

Their hasty exit did not go unnoticed.

As they weaved through the crowded restaurant, filled with patrons enjoying their meals and cocktails, hushed whispers and curious glances followed their path. The stares, coupled with the weight of the disastrous evening, pressed down on Lisa like a suffocating blanket. All she wanted was to escape into the cool night air and leave the memory of Drake, the restaurant, and the entire night behind her.

Stepping outside, Lisa drew a deep breath of the cool night air, letting it fill her lungs as if to cleanse the heaviness she felt inside. Briefly, she handed her ticket to the waiting valet, barely registering Drake catching up beside her.

"Hey, don't leave me hanging. I hate waiting. Speaking of which, I took the liberty of texting you my address," he whined before adding, “We’re going to do things your husband could never dream of. Things that might seem unfamiliar now but will become something you crave in time. Be ready, and don’t hold back.”

Lisa ignored him, her body bristling with a prickly awareness of every eye on them. Just then, the rumble of her approaching car cut through the tense silence. Relief flooded her. She practically leaped into the driver's seat, slamming the door shut behind her without a single glance in Drake's direction. With a peel of the tires, she tore out of the valet lane, leaving Drake sputtering in her dust.

Meanwhile, unseen in the shadows of a building near the restaurant, a lone figure sat hunched behind the tinted windows of a car. A camera, its faint red light a malevolent eye in the darkness, clicked silently as it captured the scene unfolding before him between Lisa and Drake. With practiced ease, the man jotted down notes.

The engine of the car purred to life as he noticed Drake climb into his car, the valet scurrying back to his post. A moment later, the taillights of Drake's car disappeared around a corner, and the man in the shadows followed suit. He merged into the flow of traffic, his car a silent predator stalking its prey. The night now held a new threat, a silent observer waiting for his moment to strike.

Chapter 16: The Crushing Blow

Steven slumped into his armchair, the soft leather molding to his weary body. His day had been an unyielding march through a maze of meetings and deadlines, a mental battlefield where focus was the only weapon. Now, as the quiet of his room enveloped him, the armor of professionalism began to crack.

The tie, a suffocating symbol of the corporate world, was the first to go. His fingers fumbled with the knot, eager to be rid of it. With a final tug, the silk fell away, landing softly on the plush carpet. His shoes, stiff and unforgiving, were the next to be discarded. They hit the floor with a dull thud, a final act of rebellion against the constraints of the day.

Exhaustion seeped into him as he peeled off his suit jacket. His reflection in the mirror was that of a stranger—eyes sunken, skin pale. The man staring back was a ghost of the confident, composed individual he'd been that morning.

A groan escaped his lips, a low, mournful sound that echoed the emptiness he felt inside. He had built a life around control, a carefully constructed fortress designed to protect him from the unpredictable tides of emotion. But in the quiet solitude of his home, the illusion crumbled, revealing the vulnerability beneath.

He had learned from a young age to control his life. That was why he was in the position he was in—a successful corporate employee, admired by peers and envied by rivals.

But somewhere along the way, the reins had slipped from his grasp. His emotions, once tightly leashed, now ran wild, a tempestuous force threatening to consume him. It was a bitter pill to swallow, the realization that the man in control was merely a facade, a carefully crafted persona designed to mask the chaos within.

Steven massaged his temples, attempting to alleviate the oncoming headache. He glanced around his room, searching for something to ground him. The accustomed surroundings offered no solace. Everything seemed to be a reminder of the control he had lost. He needed to figure things out to regain his footing before things spiraled further. The problem wasn't just at work; it was also creeping into his personal life. He knew he had to address his feelings and find a way to balance them before they overwhelmed him entirely.

The ticking of the clock seemed to mock his growing anxiety. Each second was a reminder of the time slipping away, a countdown to an unknown and, perhaps, unwelcome future. Steven knew he couldn't let this continue. He had to take back control. The thought provided sheer relief, but Steven knew the path to regaining that control was shrouded in uncertainty. His mind wandered to Lisa, a name that once brought a smile but now stirred a tempest within him. The images of their shared life now felt like shards of glass cutting into his heart. Their arguments, the pain, the *betrayal*—it all came rushing back, a persistent tide eroding the foundations of his composure.

Steven had talked to her and tried to bridge the chasm between them, but forgiveness was still a distant star. The ache of longing for her was a constant companion, a bittersweet reminder of what could have been. Yet, the fear of what might happen if he let her back into his life was equally potent. It was a dangerous game of chance, a gamble with his heart at stake.

Nausea began to grow on him, and he realized he needed to clear his head. With unsteady hands, he reached for the crystal decanter on the side table. The cool glass felt good against his skin as he poured himself a drink. The amber liquid shimmered invitingly, promising a temporary escape from the disorder within. Steven took a tentative sip, the burn of alcohol conflicting harshly with the cold ache in his chest. It was a short-lived respite from the squall raging within.

Putting down the glass, he stood and stretched, his body stiff from hours of inaction. The bed beckoned, a soft, inviting oasis. With a sigh, he put his watch on the table beside the glass and opted for a comfortable pair of pajamas. As he slipped beneath the covers, the world seemed to fade away. Sleep, a welcome oblivion, claimed him almost instantly.

After what felt like mere moments, Steven was jolted awake by the insistent flashing of his phone. A voicemail notification blinked at him, a jarring intrusion into the peaceful slumber he had finally found. He picked up the phone and unlocked it to reveal the message. The voice on the other end was familiar, the tone urgent.

It was his private investigator. A cold shiver ran down his spine.

His heart pounded in his ears. The voice sounded muffled, the words carrying a weight of urgency: "*Steven, we need to talk. I'm using a burner phone, bouncing between networks to stay off the grid. I've got something big for you. I've sent it overnight to your hotel. It's bad, Steven, really bad. I'm not where I want to be in this investigation, but I've uncovered something huge. Peter isn't who you think he is, and... Lisa... she's seeing Drake. I know, I know, it sounds crazy, but it's true. I'll keep digging, but you need to hear this. We can talk when you get back.*"

The message ended abruptly, leaving Steven suspended in a state of shock. His sleep vanished in an instant, replaced by a cold terror. He had prepared himself for the possibility of infidelity, but hearing the confirmation was a different beast entirely. His mind raced, trying to process the information. Sweat beaded on his brow as he sat bolt upright in bed, the covers tangled around his legs.

He replayed the voicemail, and as each word tumbled out, it felt as if a dagger was piercing his heart. The message sounded like a chilling confirmation of his worst fears, echoed in the quiet room. It was a betrayal on a scale he couldn't bring himself to comprehend.

"Peter isn't who I think," he whispered to himself, the words tasting like ashes on his tongue.

Steven had been so focused on his crumbling marriage, so consumed by his pain, that he hadn't questioned the broader realm of things, the hidden agendas that might be at play. *First Peter and Lisa, now...Drake and Lisa.* The realization was a bitter pill to swallow.

I need to take a step back and look at the bigger picture, Steven thought, resting his head back.

He was strong-minded and did not let his emotions dictate his next move. For now, he needed to focus on the evidence, the cold, hard facts. Until he had that in his hands, he wouldn't allow himself to be consumed by anger or despair.

With a deep breath, he tried to calm his drumming heart within, coercing himself to sleep.

The early morning light filtering through the curtains seemed almost mocking in its indifference. Sleep now felt like a distant memory. Steven's mind was a three-ring-circus of thoughts, each one more unsettling than the last. He decided he couldn't face the day—not like this. Work, a sanctuary in normal times, seemed like an alien planet now. He swung his legs over the side of the bed and stood up. The cold hardwood floor felt like a painful divergence from the warmth of the bed, a physical manifestation of the icy reality he now faced. He needed to take control and impose some semblance of order on the chaos within.

With a determined stride, he crossed the room and picked up the hotel phone. He needed to secure his professional facade to create a shield against the encroaching ordeal. Quickly dialing Sarah's number, he brought the phone to his ear.

"Hello, Mr. Blackman? The car—"

"Sarah, I'm going to be working from my room today. Please forward all calls and cancel any meetings," Steven interrupted her before she had the chance to say anything.

There was a pause on the other end, and then Sarah spoke. "Is everything okay, Mr. Blackman?"

Steven hesitated, his mind racing. "Everything's fine. I just need to focus without disruptions."

"Would you like me to bring you breakfast?"

"No, I've got the leftovers to eat in the room," he lied.

The truth was he had no appetite.

"Do you need me to come there and work today? The hotel conference room is set up—"

"No, I need you there. But thanks for asking. By the way, I'm expecting a package. It should be delivered here at the hotel. Let me know if it arrives if you happen to be here."

"No problem, sir. What time do you want lunch? Should I have it sent to your room after 12?"

"Don't worry about it. I'll order room service."

Sarah paused momentarily, her concern evident. She knew something was amiss, and he could sense it too.

"I guess let's meet when you're back at the hotel to catch up on the day," Steven said, cutting to the chase.

"Of course, Mr. Blackman. Please don't work too hard. I know you've got a lot on your plate."

"Thanks," Steven said, his voice flat.

He hung up the phone as the realization hit him: *the day ahead was going to be a long one.* He needed to focus, compartmentalize, and survive.

After some time, Steven's stomach growled, reminding him of the empty void within him. He padded over to the fridge. Inside, he found the remnants of last night's dinner: a half-eaten salad and a cold slice of pizza. It would have to do. He microwaved a cup of instant coffee, its bitter taste a harsh wake-up call.

With a makeshift breakfast consumed, Steven settled down at the small desk in the corner of the room. His laptop seemed to offer a sense of normalcy amid the disorder. He immersed himself in work. Video conferences filled the morning, and the familiar faces on the screen managed to offer a brief respite from his troubles.

As noon approached, anxiety took over him. It was time to face Mr. Weber, his demanding boss. The thought of a conference call and explaining his absence from the office and the mounting pressure was daunting. With a heavy sigh, Steven dialed his office number. The phone rang once, twice, before being answered by Sarah.

"Hello, Mr. Weber's office. Who is this speaking?"

"This is Steven Blackman. Is Mr. Weber available for a conference call?" Steven asked.

"He's in a meeting right now, Mr. Blackman. But I can have him return your call."

Relief enveloped Steven—a temporary reprieve. He could at least collect his thoughts before facing the impending conversation. Calmness seemed to infuse within him as he focused on the task at hand. He sat at the desk and overlooked the city through the cool window glass. As he reviewed an email, a knock at the door startled him.

"Yes?" he replied.

"Room service. There's a parcel for Mr. Blackman," came the muffled response.

A jolt of adrenaline shot through him—the package had arrived. His heart pounded in his chest as he rushed to the door. He yanked it open to reveal a uniformed bellhop.

"The package is marked urgent, so I thought you'd want it immediately," he explained.

Steven's hands trembled as he took the thick, neatly wrapped package. "Yes, certainly. I've been waiting for it," he said.

"Would you like to order lunch?" the bellhop asked politely.

Steven's stomach growled in agreement.

"Actually, yes. I'll have the steak sandwich and a side salad," he replied, his mind already racing ahead, eager to delve into the contents of the package.

With a nod, the bellhop retreated down the hallway. Steven closed the door behind him. He knew it was time to face the truth, whatever form it took.

A cold trepidation settled in his stomach as he tore open the package. Inside, a thick envelope lay undisturbed. With trembling hands, he extracted the contents.

The letter was brief yet damning. Steven began to read: *Mr. Blackman, the enclosed photographs document the affair between your wife and Mr. Drake. The images are arranged chronologically, with the most recent at the top.*

Steven's mind tried to process the implications of the evidence. He continued reading: *I followed Mrs. Blackman to Antonio's restaurant and observed her meeting with Mr. Drake. Subsequent surveillance revealed their movements, culminating in what I believe to be Mr. Drake's residence. These findings are preliminary, and further investigation is required-"*

The sentence was left dangling as the insistent ringing of his phone interrupted his reading. Annoyance consumed him. He glanced at the caller ID, his heart sinking as he recognized the number. Mr. Weber.

Not now.

Taking a deep breath, he answered the phone.

"Hello."

"Steven, I heard you called," Mr. Weber's voice boomed through the receiver, an unexpected burst of enthusiasm.

Steven could sense an undercurrent of excitement in his boss's voice. "Yes, I was hoping we could connect over the conference call," he replied, trying to mask his confusion.

"Oh, forget the conference call. I was just reviewing the deal, and boy, what a fine job you did. Your bonus is going to reflect just how much we appreciate your hard work."

"Thank you, Mr. Weber. I'm glad it worked out."

"Worked out? Are you kidding? It's a home run, a slam dunk! This deal is going to skyrocket our profits. The stock prices are already through the roof," Mr. Weber announced with a loud laugh.

Steven gritted his teeth. He didn't want to discuss business right now. But he knew better than to let this opportunity slip through his fingers. The praise was unexpected and presented a glimmer of positivity within the storm of his personal life. He glanced at the now-open package on the desk.

"It was a judgment call, and I'm glad it paid off. CSoft will be a great addition to the company's portfolio," he said.

"We should see some good things come out of this," Mr. Weber continued, his enthusiasm undiminished. "The last quarter's numbers weren't great, and you know how the board can be. But this deal is a game-changer. We're already talking restructuring, and I think you'd be perfect to lead the new division."

Steven's heart skipped a beat: a promotion, a new challenge, a chance to escape his current reality. But the thought of relocating to Mexico, a place he had no desire to be, filled him with unease.

"Um, I don't… Mexico isn't really my scene," Steven replied.

"I get it," Mr. Weber said understandingly and added after a pause, "So, Steven, I have been wanting to know, how'd you manage to charm Ms. Rodriguez? She's tough as nails."

The mention of Mrs. Rodriguez jolted Steven back to reality. He'd almost forgotten about their *tense* meeting.

"No magic tricks," he replied, a wry smile tugging at his lips. "Just went over the contract line by line. Laid out the pros and cons. The usual."

Mr. Weber chuckled. "Simple and effective, as always. Whatever magic you did there worked. She hasn't stopped praising you over our calls. Keep her happy; we're not out of the woods yet."

Steven forced a smile. He didn't want to think about Ms. Rodriguez or the complexities of his meeting with her. He needed to focus on the immediate crisis, which meant cutting off Mr. Weber.

"Um, Mr. Weber, I think I have another call coming up. I'll be sure to keep you updated," he paused. "I think we can wrap this up in the next week or so."

"Good man, you've got my full support. And hey, maybe bring that gorgeous wife of yours down for a visit. You two deserve a break."

Steven hesitated; the thought of involving Lisa in his professional life was a daunting prospect.

"Thanks. I'll think about it," he managed to say.

Just as he was about to end the call, a detail popped into his head. "Oh, one more thing," he said, "Ms. Rodriguez mentioned wanting to show me around the city this weekend. Not sure if it's a good idea, but you know how insistent she can be."

"Do what suits you, Steven. But be careful," Mr. Weber warned. "Things can get a little... *unpredictable* outside of the office."

"I'll be mindful of that," Steven replied.

His eyes fell on the letter he had clipped to the desk with a paperweight as he had picked up the call. Curiosity piqued his interest. He was intent on absorbing its shocking details.

"Actually, I think I should just take this call," Steven lied again.

"Sure. Talk later," Mr. Weber said, with which Steven hung up.

It was time to face whatever more awaited him.

With a deep breath, Steven reached for the letter, the paperweight cool beneath his fingertips.

His eyes scanned the words sprawled on the paper: *I wanted to get this information to you as soon as possible,* it continued. *Another person of interest here is Peter. I pulled phone records for your wife, and his number appeared frequently. I decided to look through their text messages, and my suspicions were confirmed. The texts reveal a deeper connection between them, possibly dating back to the period you three were in college, if I am right. I'm not sure what happened, but they've spent a significant amount of time together, even after college life ended.*

Steven's mind was winding. Fear and rage coiled in the pit of his stomach as he reread the words. He couldn't believe what he was reading. *Lisa and Peter connected after college?* The rational part of his brain sprinted, trying to make sense of the treachery.

How could Lisa and Peter, two people he trusted implicitly, have kept this from him for so long?

Nausea once again rose to Steven's throat. He dropped his head into his hands, the world spinning around him. He had always considered Peter a friend, a confidant. The betrayal was a bitter pill to swallow. Fear roiled within him as he continued reading the letter. The accusations were stark: *Mrs. Blackman and Peter's phones were frequently in proximity, often near his home when he was absent.*

Swiftly, Steven clicked on the calendar on his laptop and compared the dates to his business trips.

No, no. This can't be it.

Each absence was a potential opening for their disloyalty—the evidence directed toward his shattered trust.

The realization hit him with the force of a physical blow. Every carefully constructed facet of his life felt like a house of cards crumbling before his eyes. The magnitude of the deceit was overwhelming. Anger, sadness, and disbelief consumed him all at once, each emotion fighting for dominance as Steven sat motionless, the letter trembling in his grip. His chest felt tight, his mind spiraling with questions that had no answers. The betrayal was unbearable—Drake's affair with Lisa was devastating enough, but to now confront the possibility of his childhood best friend's deception felt like a dagger driven straight to his core.

He thought he had faced the worst. He thought he had seen the full picture. But as his eyes darted back to the letter, something shifted in his mind. A small, insistent thought pushed its way through the chaos, demanding his attention.

Drake.

Steven's breath tethered as he leaned back, staring blankly at the ceiling. His sharp mind, always adept at piecing together puzzles, had been too clouded by rage to see it earlier. As the pieces began to align, a dark realization clawed its way to the surface.

Drake wasn't just any man having an affair with Lisa. No, Drake was sharp—too *sharp*. His cunning was legendary within their organization. They worked in a field where every player was a strategist, where every move was calculated, and where weakness was exploited. Drake didn't stumble blindly into an affair with an employee's wife without a deeper reason.

What if this wasn't about love or lust at all? What if this relationship was an intentionally crafted plot to bring him down?

The thought gripped Steven, cold and unrelenting. His hand tightened around the corner of the desk as he thought back to Drake's smirks in meetings, the subtle digs disguised as humor, the way he always seemed a step ahead. Steven had dismissed it before as professional rivalry, the kind that came with ambitious men competing in the same arena. But now, it felt different. It felt personal.

Sweat beaded on Steven's forehead as the implications sunk in. Drake wasn't innocent enough to pursue Lisa without knowing more about her life—her secrets. Steven's gut twisted as a new thought struck him with the force of a blow.

Did Drake know about Lisa and Peter long before the news came to him?

Steven's pulse quickened. Drake had resources—resources not unlike Steven's own. If Steven could hire an investigator from military intelligence, so could Drake. The man wasn't impulsive; he was deliberate, precise. He observed every angle, studied every variable, and measured every consequence before making a move. However, Steven was more concerned with his wife than his work rival—who was equally involved individual in this affair.

His breathing grew shallow as he rubbed his temple, trying to keep his varying thoughts under control. *Could he have failed as a husband?* Lisa, his golden girl, was often seen as a prize he had won. But had he ever truly done justice to their relationship? Had he become so consumed with his work that he'd pushed her into the arms of another?

His thoughts spiraled further. *Had he let his attraction to Sofia Rodriguez blur his own moral boundaries?* Steven knew his fleeting moments of interest in Sofia were nothing compared to Lisa's betrayals, but they weren't inconsequential either.

The letter slipped from his hand, fluttering to the desk. For a moment, the force of it all seemed unbearable. But then he forced himself to take a deep breath. He couldn't let his emotions take over. Not yet. Confronting Lisa, Peter, or Drake, now would only lead to chaos. He needed time to think. Perhaps this was an opportunity—a chance to reclaim what was his and rebuild what had been broken.

Just then, his phone buzzed. The screen lit up with Lisa's name.

Steven froze, his thumb moving over the screen. His mind screamed at him to ignore it, to give himself time. But his heart, heavy with doubt and longing, told him otherwise.

He answered. "Lisa?"

Her voice came through the line, hesitant but familiar. "Steven? Can you hear me?"

Tears pooled in Steven's eyes. A part of him wanted to confront her, to demand answers. But another part—the more logical part—knew that this was his chance to take control, to reshape their marriage and move forward. Perhaps this was a sign, a moment of grace to make things right.

"Yes," he said. "I hear you."

Lisa hesitated. "Is everything okay? You've been distant. I thought I'd check in… I've been missing you."

Steven swallowed hard, his emotions warring within him. "I miss you too, Lisa. I just… I've had a lot on my mind."

"Work again?" she asked with a faint chuckle.

Steven let out a small laugh, though it was devoid of humor. "Work. Life. Everything."

"Well, I was missing you," Lisa said softly. "So, I thought I'd call."

Steven felt a lump in his throat. "I want to come home, Lisa. I want to see you. Just us. Maybe… maybe we can get away for a while."

Her laughter bubbled through the phone. “Steven, is work finally breaking you?”

“Everything is,” he admitted quietly. “I just need you.”

There was a pause, and Steven imagined the faint smile he knew was spreading across her face.

“When are you coming back?” she asked.

“Soon,” he promised. “I just need to tie up some things here, and then I’ll be all yours.”

“All mine?” she teased.

Steven’s lips curved into a smile. “All yours.”

For the first time in weeks, a drop of calm took over him completely. Maybe this was the turning point that would allow him to finally escape the web of deception and betrayal that had entangled his life.

As Lisa’s laughter echoed gently through the line, Steven allowed himself to hope. Perhaps this was his way forward—a chance to amend his life, his marriage, and himself. But in the back of his mind, the questions about Drake and Peter remained, lurking like a shadow he couldn’t shake.

For now, though, Steven pushed them aside. He would deal with confronting them later.

Right now, Lisa was waiting.

Why?

I often wondered why life sometimes must change,
when you do all you can, yet your heart still feels so blue...
Was I doing my best to keep everything the same,
or is this just something my heart always knew...

Right now, this moment, I feel the colossal raindrops,
fallen upon my head, with my life a complete mess...
I don't know what I have done, but I'm praying it stops,
please let it subside, this pain I can't express...

I'm in a place where the sun refuses to shine,
and I can't see past this moment of pain...
It's like everything I search for, I just can't find,
it's like the stars in the sky will not align,

I know that in life, there are things we go through,
even while pretending. I need to press on...
God, you are the only one that knows this just isn't true,
answer me...why don't you make it all be gone...

In my heart of hearts, I know just what I must do,
but I need the strength to make everything alright...
Lord, I ask you to forgive me, I ask this of you,
to get through just one more night...

I know what I must do...

Made in the USA
Columbia, SC
25 June 2025

13ebb3cb-4296-4e04-95b5-7a59a6a5dc74R01